AMERICAN MASCULINE

★ ★ ★ ★ ★

AMERICAN MASCULINE

STORIES

SHANN RAY

Graywolf Press

This publication is made possible by funding provided in part by a grant from the
Minnesota State Arts Board, through an appropriation by the Minnesota State
Legislature, a grant from the National Endowment for the Arts, and private funders.
Significant support has also been provided by Target; the McKnight Foundation;
and other generous contributions from foundations, corporations, and individuals.
To these organizations and individuals we offer our heartfelt thanks.

Published by Graywolf Press
250 Third Avenue North, Suite 600
Minneapolis, Minnesota 55401

All rights reserved.

www.graywolfpress.org

Published in the United States of America

ISBN 978-1-55597-588-3

2 4 6 8 9 7 5 3 1
First Graywolf Printing, 2011

Library of Congress Control Number: 2011923187

Cover design: Kapo Ng @ A-Men Project
Cover photo: Oli Gardner

For Jennifer

So every day
I was surrounded by the beautiful crying forth
of the ideas of God,

one of which was you.
— Mary Oliver

CONTENTS

INTRODUCTION

THE SENTENCES IN THIS BOOK have such grace and mus-
cularity that they seem more performed than written, and the
author's images and events carry the nearly visceral weight of
memory. In fact, during the weeks immediately following my
initial reading of *American Masculine,* I twice caught myself strug-
gling with what I thought was personal recollection only to realize that it was actually an episode from one of the stories. For
example, I thought I had dreamt of a train and I was trying to
describe to a friend how compelling the dream had been when
I realized that it was not a dream locomotive but the train from
"The Great Divide" curling about my consciousness, nosing its
way into my life, making claims on my experience. The work
has that kind of resonance. You finish each story with the understanding that something meaningful has happened to you,
and though you may not be able to specify the meaning, you
understand nonetheless that you have lived through something
powerful and significant.

In terms of certain formal aspects of composition, one might
call several of the stories in *American Masculine* experimental,
much as one might accurately call the stories of Alice Munro experimental. It is part of the magic of Munro's stories that they
never *seem* experimental no matter how inventively they are struc-
tured or how radically they are shaped. In like fashion, Shann
Ray's stories do not *feel* experimental. In fact, they feel almost
old-fashioned, written with unfashionable seriousness and the
kind of multidimensional characters that become forcefully real
to the reader precisely because they escape easy definition. These

characters are rich and fully imagined, and like real people, they are also mysterious and elusive.

American Masculine is a powerful, resonant work of literature, and Shann Ray is a masterful and original writer.

ON JUDGING THE CONTEST

What one hopes for when judging a contest is that one entry will stand out like a giant above the rest, and the only difficulty one will have is finding an adequate stepladder to complete the coronation. And so I was simultaneously distressed and delighted to find that of the ten finalists for the Bakeless Prize, eight were goliaths worthy of publication, praise, and admiration. I was distressed because I knew that all but one of these worthy books would not be awarded the prize, and because I had so much work yet to do to choose among them, and at the same time I was delighted because the work entailed rereading such fine works of fiction. After a second read of each, I narrowed the list to three, and I ultimately chose one. It is the best of a very strong lot, and I am grateful to the preliminary judges who screened the manuscripts and selected from the many hundreds of entries the ten outstanding works that arrived on my doorstep in a mammoth and utterly daunting cardboard box. Screening manuscripts in such contests is difficult, demanding, and thankless work, and so I'd like to offer them thanks by name: Will Allison, Lauren Groff, Skip Horack, Alex Espinoza, Aryn Kyle, Kirsten Menger-Anderson, Matthew Pitt, Salvatore Scibona, and Steve Wingate. You have my gratitude, as do Jennifer Bates and Michael Collier, for their patience, kindness, and goodwill. Thanks also to Graywolf Press for its commitment to the publication of literature.

Robert Boswell

AMERICAN MASCULINE

—for Cleveland Highwalker, my father's good friend, gone now

HOW WE FALL

BENJAMIN KILLSNIGHT sat in the easy chair in his living room after dark, clear amber drink in hand. He stared straight ahead. She was out getting bent again, while he stayed home. He'd lived in Billings for some time, young and strong in the city, director of youth programs for the downtown YMCA, Northern Cheyenne, and proud. But being away from his people he had to admit he'd gone wrong. Urban time was all speed, nothing like rez time, and he hadn't gained a taste for it, even if he was well liked in city league basketball and at work and nearly everywhere he went.

Grandson of Raymond Killsnight, he'd borrowed his grandfather's elk-bone breastplate, framed it in a shadow box and placed it over the cherrywood mantle of the fireplace next to the small black-framed picture of his grandpa in full regalia. His grandfather's face looked out at him, strong and hard like the face of a mountain. Benjamin had aligned five white colonnade candles on the tile below the mantle and now their bright fires shone in the dark like a small upside-down sky.

In America, he thought, if you were to be a man, and if you wanted a woman, you borrowed boldness. Each man had it to varying degrees, the verve that drew women, the force, the facade, the dream with which he governed his own interplay of looks and presence and urgency. Benjamin lived in a small house, seven hundred square feet, down in the tight-fit tracts a couple of blocks south of Montana Avenue and back west again toward I-90. He thought of his wife, Sadie. For her he'd always had nothing but urgency.

THE NEXT DAY near dusk he drove slow on I-90 past the oil refinery, a bit delirious from the vodka he'd taken from his cache in the fill water of the toilet at work. Even lifting the back you couldn't see the bottle, label-less, there under the buoy. He drove east toward the Dakotas, away from all the lights, the refinery's night fires. Exultant and married at twenty-three, he was one of the Beautiful People, an athlete, and in the seat next to him in the burn of sundown was his white woman wife, made like a feather, shaft of bones and thin body illumined. Her face to the side, she stared out the window as the freeway set itself along the gunmetal gray of the river. He wanted to find a turnout somewhere between here and I-94. Park the car. Look at the river. Drink together.

He'd seen three friends die his senior year at St. Labre, the Catholic school thirty miles east of Lame Deer, on the edge of the reservation. Joe Big Head hung himself in his own bedroom, Elmore Running Dog was knifed in the chest in broad daylight, and Michael Bear Below was shot with a high-powered rifle at a party in Plenty Coups on the Crow rez. The bullet pierced the skull and killed him instantly. He'd known them all since kindergarten. He looked at Sadie in the passenger seat and knew she struggled with life and with herself and he wondered what kept her alive. After his father's death from alcohol he had no mother to speak of, and thinking of it he always felt dark. Sadie, for her part, had no father. Different lives, same story.

Even Benjamin's grandfather Leonard had taken the tribe's

money, boarded a train on the Hi-Line bound for Spokane, and never returned. In a different light, when Benjamin left the rez he borrowed his father's swagger, the way he could look the white man in the eye and smile, drunk or not, and it led Benjamin to an associate arts degree from Miles Community College in Miles City, where he'd played shooting guard, and then to a BA in physical education from Eastern Montana College in Billings.

Benjamin had been a drinker since an uncle started him on it in grade school. Same uncle forced a drunk Sioux woman on him when Ben was thirteen and he had run from the house, crying from her terrible fingers.

SCANNING THE RIVER from a lookout near the frontage road, Sadie drunk and gone in his lap, Benjamin made what seemed like an unlikely pact with heaven—with the Holy Spirit, she'd say if she was awake; the Great Spirit, he'd counter and they'd smile. A pistol of verve and fire: that was Sadie. She didn't care who she spoke to, or what about. She was thin and fast and beautiful, and seeing her passed out again sobered him. He brushed the hair back to see her face. Hard to hold, that one. Elusive as the wind. But he loved her like he loved wilderness. She was made of untame things, and mystery. So right then and there he vowed to stop drinking.

It took three years to celebrate his first full year of sobriety, and when it happened he called his brother, Titus, back in Lame Deer to tell him. Benjamin had gotten a monkey fist from his sponsor that night, a leather necklace with a small leather knot signifying a year free. Sadie wasn't into it. "Parched, enit," Titus said, laughing, then he said, "I got a daughter now." He said it so quiet Benjamin wasn't sure he heard.

"A daughter?" Benjamin said, rolling the monkey fist between thumb and forefinger.

"Yeah," Titus answered. "Her name is Elsie."

A daughter, thought Benjamin, I'm her uncle, and when he hung up the phone he opened his front door. He wanted to whoop at the top of his lungs. Instead he clenched his fists to his chest and said under his breath, "Yes!"

IN WINTER of that year Benjamin caught Sadie sleeping with his best friend from high school, Jack Plenty Buffalo, who was visiting from Lame Deer. Benjamin threw Jack naked out the back door, beat him unconscious, and broke out three of his teeth. Sadie revived Jack and that night Benjamin forgave all like a good rez boy and relapsed, sucking beer and Canadian whiskey from a plastic bottle with Sadie and Jack until past two, sometimes laughing and hacking so hard he cried. In the morning Jack left and two nights later Benjamin drove Montana Avenue and cut down across the river and out into the river valley to attend the AA meeting in a back room at the Christian Missionary Alliance Church, set like a small barn in the fields. His wife, head high, face like a flint, accompanied him.

He worked on small hopes, and limited understanding. When he walked, the details came to his brain cleaner and less muddied, the outline of an aspen on the rise below the rim rock, the way the river met the riverbed and banked away south.

A month into his second real sobriety he found Sadie naked and passed out on the couch with a recent AA group member named Richard. Benjamin was more prepared this time. He left a note in the bathroom saying, *I love you, Sadie. I want to stay married to you. Are you willing to give up drinking?* He left the house and ate dinner with his sponsor, a man with thirty years' sobriety who was a member of the Spokane Tribe. Afterward they stood outside his sponsor's van and lit sweetgrass and prayed together and when Benjamin came home at 11:00 p.m. Sadie was gone. Her own message, placed on his pillow, written in clean blue cursive on a yellow pastel sticky note, said *I'm sorry.*

* * *

FOR HER PART, Sadie took the small stash of money they had and bought a bus ticket to Seattle. When she arrived she went to Pike Place Market and panhandled enough change to buy three bottles of cheap wine, drinking each one quickly until she passed out on the grass in a public square overlooking the Sound. Unconscious, she was arrested and carried to jail.

She woke on a hard metal bench inside a holding cell and stared at the wall and whispered, "He was nothing to me." She bit at her cuticles, making them bleed. Her face felt swollen. We hide behind our faces, she thought, we make our faces like armor. She went from jail to a homeless shelter for women where the state let her work off her fine and when she'd paid her debt she wandered out into the night where in a dark low-ceilinged bar she found a job as a cocktail waitress. She passed like a day-ghost between the shelter and the bar until she'd made enough money for a one-room apartment in the flats south of downtown. She worked, kept the apartment clean, and drank at least two pints a day.

After nearly a year, and a string of men, she was kicked out for not paying rent. She kept working and drinking and went back to living at the shelter, where she slept during the day and rose at night, and it was on one of these nights that a man approached her in the dark hull of the bar and said, I've been watching you, and she said, Thanks, and when the night ended she went with him to his single-wide trailer in the slipshod housing, disjointed, largely colorless, south of the industrial zone. The place seemed smaller inside, single dim light from the kitchen. It felt good to forget, though she knew it amounted only to emptiness. Lying together, drunk and high, his question barely registered . . . "You said you were married. Tell me about your husband?"

"He is nothing to me," she repeated.

In the early morning she touched a thin sheen of water in the bottom of the kitchen sink. She moved her index finger in a cursive pattern and wrote Benjamin's full name, then erased it, then wrote her own name. The nature of the lines and their slow evaporation worked at her like a thing that gnawed bone. Life is no solace, she told herself, and went back to bed.

She kept on this way for six months, before she left the man and the job the same day and walked among the abandoned store-fronts downtown where she shuffled her feet and panhandled and drank until she found an alcove in an alley she thought lent enough shelter to avoid being taken to jail again. She leaned a long slab of soiled cardboard over her body and slept. Night following day she trudged and slept and put down liquor and gathered a little food. She traded clothes once at the House of Charity off Royal Street downtown, continuing this way for near a month undiscovered. At the end of it she walked into the public restroom in the small park above the Alaska Way Viaduct. She stared at her face, pocked and streaked with dirt. Her eyes looked foreign and blown out.

Just outside the bathroom a middle-aged white man in a pin-striped business suit propositioned her, saying he'd pay for favors. She refused and walked back into the bathroom. She took off her coat, a light windbreaker she'd kept since Billings, then removed her shirt and her skirt and used the hand soap to wash her upper body, her face, her hair. She put her head beneath the hand dryer and dried her hair, combing it with her fingers. She took her clothes and worked the larger blemishes by rubbing the soap to a lather, rinsing each stain and repeat-ing the process until the clothing looked respectable. She dried her shirt and skirt and coat under the hand dryer. When it was done she folded the coat neatly, put her clothes back on and tucked the shirt in and looked at herself in the mirror again. The shirt was dark blue, too large, shapeless. The skirt was out-dated, but decent. Long-sleeved shirt, long skirt; they covered her bruises well enough. Her face seemed not her own but at least it wasn't filthy anymore.

She strode outside and walked to the area downtown where the glass and metal glowed and the people came in droves from their high-powered jobs. Happy hour, they'd stop in the bars before going home. She'd have to work fast with the city ordinance that disallowed panhandling . . . police roaming like predators. There were a good twenty or thirty bars in the business sector. She only needed a little. She approached the kind-faced ones first, but later, indiscriminate, she confronted everyone she encountered. Laying out her hands she said, "Please, can I have some money? I'm trying to get home." Same lines. Sincerely delivered. Mostly she received nothing, but some gave more than others, and that's all she'd need, just some. At the end of two hours she had eighty-three dollars and change. She needed more. She saw a woman dressed all in gold, walking with two friends, laughing, smiling. Sadie approached and said "Please," and the woman barely looked at her and gave her a hundred dollar bill and walked on.

Sadie stared at the bill in her hand, then at the woman advancing up the sidewalk. Already a half a block away the woman walked unconcerned, as if nothing had passed between them. "Thank you," Sadie whispered, and she turned and walked south and west again.

Among the superstructures that towered over her, Sadie tramped toward the Sound, the last light of day awash in the street, a huge cold light that turned buildings and cars and people pink, as if everyone blushed, she thought. As if everyone was ashamed, and everyone beautiful. She entered the Greyhound depot and took the night bus to Billings on a weekday special for eighty dollars. When she arrived the following night she walked from the depot through the stunted buildings of downtown Billings, below the hospitals, and into the city to the YMCA. She peered in the front window for a moment but kept moving and walked to the Amtrak station just past First. From the phone booth near the door she thought she might

call Benjamin but thought better of it. She boarded the North
Coast Hiawatha at 10:00 a.m. and rode nineteen hours, arriving
in Minneapolis aching and hungry, her cravings awake and rave-
nous like animals. She sat down near the drinking fountain in
the station and wiped the sweat from her forehead and drank as
much water as she could. She filled her stomach. She knew she
couldn't arrive drunk. She walked most of the day, panhandled
some, and took the last stretch by cab.

Her mother taught accounting at the University of Minnesota,
and most of what Sadie remembered of childhood with her was
austere and severe, but when Sadie knocked on the door and her
mother answered, her mother's face broke and she put her arms
around Sadie's neck and wept. Sadie stood blank as her mother
held her, and said nothing as her mother kissed her face. "Are
you okay?" her mother said, gripping Sadie's shoulders, speaking into her eyes. "I've missed you. I thought you were dead."
Sadie stared at her.

"You're alive!" she said, kissing her forehead. "I've missed you
so much, Sadie. I love you."

Sadie didn't respond and her mother led her to the kitchen
and prepared tea for her and wrapped her in a comforter and sat
next to her and held her hand. She made a grilled cheese sandwich for her, and sliced some apples, and afterward she walked
her to the bathroom and when Sadie was ready she led her to the
guest bed and tucked her in and covered the bed with blankets.
Sadie stared out as if from a cave. Her eyes focused on the spare
nakedness of the room. No pictures. Blank walls. Blankets of solid
color with no pattern. Near her head a square night table, a simple
lamp. The burgundy shade looked like a small well-lit house.

Her mother slid in next to her and stroked Sadie's hair until
she fell asleep.

HER MOTHER waited until Sadie started to find her feet again.
They were at the kitchen table over tea. Her mother held the

picture in her hand, a photo Sadie had managed to keep with
her through everything.

"Your husband?" she asked, holding it up, staring. He wore
jeans and a T-shirt, arms folded, legs crossed as he leaned against
the hood of a Camaro. "Handsome," she said. "Very handsome."

"Was he good to you?" her mother asked.

"Yes," Sadie said. She looked at her mother. "He meant something." Sadie went quiet. They watched each other. Her mother
ran her fingers through Sadie's hair.

DAYS INTO DAYS. A year, two years, more. Benjamin hadn't
heard a thing.

At night in the subtle glow from the dash lights, he drove
alone among the fast-moving cars and his mind returned to
Sadie. She'd been too open-handed and easy, and he harsh, too
fragile. She was gone a very long time. He hadn't saved himself.
No illusions. They'd lasted some he had to admit, but even at
the end of it, sober as he wanted to be, they were poison to each
other. He'd grown too rigid and couldn't stand her running to
the bars. He thought of his eyes on alcohol, gray coals in a brick-
like face, a vicious mouth that lifted flesh from bone like a man
field-dressed a deer. He'd eyed her often with ugliness and mis-
direction, his lips pursed, his look piercing and cruel—and now
on the other side of the divide his only hope despite how he'd
been back then was to be different. He'd be tenderhearted this
time, ready to change. If he could find a real woman he'd do well
by her. The children they had would sleep like bears, and wake
powerful in the world.

He'd never find that woman.

Driving, he checked himself. What did he know, really? I don't
know anything, he thought, about anyone. Even knowing himself seemed like a joke. He'd just keep driving to AA like he had
for some time, good meeting in the conference room of an old
hotel on Twenty-seventh up toward the airport, precise regimen,

daily. He'd had other women. He thought of them sometimes. He
tried not to think of Sadie. He'd been training his mind to quit
doubting, quit tempting darkness. If he tried he could reach past
the self-loathing, find a way to hold her and himself in a good
light, perhaps the whole world in a good light. His sponsor had
him practicing most nights on the drive home. Forget about her,
they all said, everyone in the group. He was healthy now. Good
job. No drugs. No booze. Still, she unraveled him.

Often, as he drove, his hands went wet as rain and he imagined himself as a young boy entering a strange house in the
Heights. As if in a dream, he saw his mother standing before him
gripped about the neck by a large white man and forced to watch
as an ugly white woman approached her. The white woman will
be brutal to her, he thought. She will beat her. Then a name would
come to him, it was his mother's name, or a name given to her,
Little Bird, and he couldn't remember how she received this name,
and as soon as he remembered the name the dream changed and
it was only him with his mother and he held her head and kissed
her cheek and said kind words to her.

When he thought right his hands didn't sweat. He knew then
he'd gotten past the fear because his mind opened up and his
face felt more together, not so loose. Driving, he'd picture himself
in the last evening of summer, in a modest home outside Lame
Deer. He saw a woman, but always, her head was turned. They'd
be lying down in a large bed, him watching her sleep, her artistic
body and fine lines; a real woman, and he a real man, and there in
the waking dream he saw himself clearly. He walked alone in the
fields of her loveliness and he beckoned her and she turned and
still he could not quite make out her face, but it was not weary,
and in her eyes was a promise and he saw that her look was gra-
cious and the touch of her hand was meant for him, and he felt
his burdens fall away, the weight of his failings become as nothing. *Nehmehohtahts,* he whispered in Cheyenne, I love you—and

in the warmth of their bed in the half-world between sleep and morning he reached to caress the elusive nature of her ways and into her presence she welcomed him, and the words from her lips came softly in the darkness.

I have loved you with an everlasting love, I have drawn you with loving-kindness.

At night in his bed he fell asleep and dreamed, and hoped he wouldn't wake.

HE WOKE in daylight to the sound of a phone ringing, a slight sound he hardly heard from the other room, and he rose and walked down the hall, seven years sober, seven single. On the phone, quiet, came Sadie's voice. We borrow dignity, Benjamin thought, or we borrow disgrace. She was calling from a phone booth on the corner of First and North Thirtieth down by Montana Avenue. He made himself ready. He wore his best shirt.

They hadn't spoken since she left. He didn't know where she'd gone.

He drove to find her and they went together and sat in a booth at Frank's Diner near the river and she told him she'd moved back with her mother in Minnesota, said she'd been sober three years, seven months, seven days. Her work as a dental hygienist had been consistent and good. She didn't contact him because she didn't trust herself.

"And if I said I'm with someone else?" he said.

His eyes burned into her. She looked to the window. "I'd be happy for you," she said. "And sad for me." She turned to him again. She didn't look away.

Her sincerity broke him. His voice failed. She stared at him. "I'm not with someone else," he said.

IN MONTANA on the high steppe below the great mountains the birds called raptors fly long and far, and with their

translucent predatory eyes they see for miles. The Blackfeet called
it the backbone of the world. Once he watched two golden eagles
sweeping from the pinnacled heights, the great stone towers. He
was three hours from Billings, west past Bozeman. The day was
crisp, the sky free of clouds, the sun solitary and white at the zenith. Hunting whitetail he sat on his heels, his rifle slung across
his back as he glassed the edge of coulees and the brush that
lined the fields. He used the binoculars with focused precision,
looking for the crowns of bucks that would be lying down, hiding. But it was up high to his right, along the granite ridge of the
nearest mountain, where he'd seen movement.

He recognized the birds and set the glasses on them and saw
distinctly their upward arc far above the ridgeline. He followed
them as they reached an impossibly high apex where they turned
and drew near each other and with a quick strike locked talons
and fell. The mystery, he thought, simple as that, the bright maj-
esty of all things. They gripped one another and whirled downward, cumbersome and powerful and elegant. He followed them
all the way down and at last the ground came near and they
broke and seemed suddenly to open themselves and catch the
wind again and lift. Their wings cleaved the air as they climbed
steadily until at last they opened wide and caught the warm ther-
mals that sent them with great speed arcing above the mountain.
There they dipped for a moment, then rose again on vigorous
wingbeats all the way to the top of the sky where they met one
another and held each other fiercely and started all over, falling
and falling.

—for Charlie Calf Robe, Honey Davis, and James Welch

THE GREAT DIVIDE

The train moves west on the Hi-Line outside Browning, tight-bound in an upward arc along the sidewall of tremendous mountains, the movement of metal and muscle working above the treeline, chugging out black smoke. Smoke, black first against the grayish rock, the granite face of the mountain, then higher and farther back black into the keen blue of sky without clouds.

1

THE BOY five years old and big, bull child his father calls him, and bulls he rides, starting at six on the gray old man his father owns, then at nine years and ten in the open fields of neighboring ranches. He enters his first real rodeo at thirteen in Glasgow and on from there, three broken fingers, a broken ankle, broken clavicle, and a cracked wrist bone. Otherwise unharmed, he knows the taste of blood, fights men twice his age while going to bars with his father. When he loses, his father grows quiet, cusses him when they get home, beats him. When he wins, his father praises him.

Work, his father says, because you ain't getting nothing. People are takers. As well shoot you as look at you.

At school he has high marks. He desires to please his mother.

Home, he smells the gun cleaning, the oil, the parts in neat rows on the kitchen table. The table is long and rectangular, of rough-hewn wood she drapes in white cloth. He sees the elongated pipe cleaner, the blackened rags, the sheen of rifle barrel, the worn wood of stock. He hears the word *Winchester* and the way his father speaks it, feels his father's look downturned, his father's eyes shadowed, submerged in the bones, the flesh of the face. The family inhabits a one-room ranch house, mother, father, son. There is a plankwood floor, an eating space, a bed space, cook stove. A small slant-roofed barn stands east of the house where the livestock gather in the cold. Mother is in bed saying, Don't make a mess. The boy's father, meticulous at the table, says, Quiet woman. Outside, the flat of the high plains arcs toward Canada. To the south the wild wind blows snow from here to a haze at the earth's end. A rim of sun, westerly, is red as blood.

The boy's mother reads aloud by lamplight. Looking up, into his eyes, Mind your schooling, she says. She touches his face. The words she reads go out far, they encompass the world, and in the evening quiet the boy and his father curl at her feet on the bed listening. Before I formed you in the womb I knew you, she reads, and before you were born I set you apart.

In town the boy witnesses a drunken Indian pulled from his horse by a group of four men. Hard rain falling, the boy standing on the boardwalk staring out. The man has wandered from the Sioux reservation, Assiniboine, day ride toting liquor, empty, seeking more. They throw his body to the ground, press down his head. Their hands are knotted in his hair and into the wet earth they push his face until it's gone. They throw loud words from white-red mouths while the Indian's body lurches and moves beneath them. The man's lathered voice seeks life and they laugh and champion each other before they rise and spit and walk away. The Indian turns his head to the side and breathes. The boy waits. He lifts the man, positions him on his horse. The boy slaps the round flank and horse and rider continue on. The boy watches, cleans his hands on his pants and when he turns he is violently struck down in the street.

His father stands over him and holds the shovel, the long handle he put to the boy's head, the father's countenance as misshapen as the mud that holds the boy, the boy's blood. Sir? The boy says. You helped the Indian, his father says, and swings the handle again in a fine circular motion that opens a straight clean gash above the boy's cheekbone. The boy lowers his head. He touches the wound, dirtying it, feeling it fill and flow. His eyes are down. He keeps silent. Next time finish it, his father says. The father leaves him lie. The boy follows him home. Voiceless, they work the land, the boy in his father's shadow from the dawn, walking. The sound of his mother is what he carries when he goes.

Sixteen years old, the boy walks the fenceline in a whiteout. He is six foot seven inches tall. He weighs two hundred and fifty pounds. Along a slight game trail on the north fence he is two hours from the house at thirty below zero. He wonders about his father, gone three days. His father had come back from town with a flat look on his face. He'd sat on the bed and wouldn't eat. At dark he'd made a simple pronouncement. Getting food, he said, then gripped the rifle, opened the door, and strode outside long legged against the bolt of wind and snow. Gone.

Walking, the boy figures what he's figured before and this time the reckoning is true. He sees the black barrel of the rifle angled on the second line of barbed wire, snow a thin mantle on the barrel's eastward lie. He sees beneath it the body-shaped mound, brushes the snow away with a hand, finds the frozen head of his father, the open eyes dull as gray stones. A small hole under the chin is burnt around the edges, and at the back of his father's head, fist-sized, the boy finds the exit wound.

When the boy pulls the gun from his father's hand two of the fingers snap away and land in the snow. The boy opens his father's coat, puts the fingers in his father's front shirt pocket. He shoulders his father, carries the gun, takes his father home. The boy's face is a tangle of deep-set lines. Where he walks, the land runs to the end of the eye and meets a sky pale as bone.

They lay him on the floor under the kitchen table. At the gray opening of dawn the boy positions old tires off behind the house, soaks them in gasoline and lights them, oily-red pyres and slanted smoke columns stark in the winter quiet. The ground thaws as the boy waits. He spends morning to evening, using his father's pickax, then the shovel, and still they bury the body shallow. He pushes the earth in over his father, malformed rock fused with ice and soil, and when he's done the boy pounds the surface with the flat back of the shovel, loud bangs that sound blunt and hard in the cold. The snow is light now, driven by wind on a slant from the north. His mom forms a crude cross of root wood from the cellar and the boy manipulates the rock, positioning the cross at the head of the grave. The boy removes his broken felt cowboy hat, his gloves. His mom reaches, holds the boy's hand. Their faces turn raw in the cold. Dead now, she says. Your father saw the world darkly, and people darker still. Find the good, boy. She squeezes the boy's hand, Dust to dust. May the Good Lord make the crooked paths straight, the mountains to be laid low, the valleys to rise, and may the Lord do with the dead as He wills.

Already inside the boy a will is growing, he feels it, abstruse, sullen, a chimera of two persons, the man of violence at odds with the angel of peace. Find the good, the boy thinks.

The next day, sheriff and banker come and say I'm sorry and the four ride in the cab of the Studebaker back to town. Papers and words, the ranch is taken, some little money granted and the two move thirty miles to Sage, farther yet toward the northeast edge of Montana, the town joined to the straight rail track that runs the Hi-Line. Small town, Sage. Post office, two bars, general store. They room with an old woman near dead in a house with floors that shine of maple, neat-lined hardwood in every room.

At night the boy hears a howling wind that blends to the whistle of the long train, the ground rumble of the tracks, the walls like a person afraid, shaking, the bed moving, the bones in him jarred, and listening he is drifting, asleep, lost on a flat-board bunk near the ceiling in a dark compartment, carried far into forested lands. Within the year, the boy's mom dies. In the morning under cover of cotton sheet and colored quilt he finds her quiet and still. He lays himself down next to her, holds her frail body in his arms and shakes silently as he weeps. In the end he stands and leans over her and kisses her forehead. In her hair, the small ivory comb given by the boy's father nearly two decades before. The boy places the comb in his breast pocket. In her hand he finds a page torn from scripture, Isaiah in her fingers of bone, the hollow of her hand, the place that was home to the shape of his face. He lifts the page, finds her weary under-line, *Arise, shine, for your light has come. And the glory of the Lord has arisen upon you. Behold, darkness covers the earth, and deep darkness its people, but the glory of the Lord has arisen upon you.*

The boy waits. He stays where he is, not knowing. Behind the Mint Bar past midnight, he beats a man fresh from the rail line until the man barely breathes. When it started the man had cussed the boy and called him outside. The boy followed, not caring. The man's face was clean, white as an eggshell, but the boy made it purple, a dark oblong bruise engorged above the man's neckline. She has been dead one month now.

The boy lies on the hardwood floor at the house in Sage watching the elderly landlady as she enters the front door. She is methodical as she works the lock with gnarled fingers. Welcome, ma'am, he mouths the words. Same to you boy, she answers. Same hour each day she returns from the post office. It is dusk. The boy sees the woman's face, the boned-out look she

wears. They have their greeting, she passes into the kitchen, he
notices the light, a white form reflected left-center in the front
window of the old woman's house. The house faces away from
the town's main street. The thing is a quirk, he thinks, a miracle
of fluked architecture that pulls the light more than one hundred feet from across the alley and down the street, from the
pointed apex of the general store and its hollow globe-shaped
street lamp beneath which the night people ebb and flow on the
boardwalk. The light comes through the aperture of a window
at the top of the back stairs. From there it hits a narrow gold-
framed mirror in the hallway and sends its thin icon into the
wide living room. The light is morphed as it sits on the front
glass, an odd-shaped sphere almost translucent at dusk, then
bright white, bony as a death's head by the time of darkness.
The boy hears the woman on the stairs, her languid gate, the
creaking ascent to her room. As her body passes, the light disap-
pears then returns. She is never in the front room at night and
the boy rarely looks at her during the day, done as he is over his
mother, over the loss of all things.

A man will be physical, he thinks, forsake things he should
never have forsaken, his kin, himself, the ground that gave him
life. Death will be the arms to hold him, the final word to give
him rest.

The boy curls inward, continues to lie on the floor for days.
The greeting remains the same, the woman leaves him his space.
He pictures the round bulb over the general store, pictures himself beneath it in the dirt street where he stands in the deep night
and looks up. He beholds the bloom of light as he might a near
star, a sun. Then he sees himself above it, behind it, clenching
the roof between his knees as he would a circus horse, his chest
upraised, his father's big sledgehammer lifted overhead. He pulls
down sky with arms like wedges. He blasts the light to smither-
eens. He floats in shards of glass and frozen light, soft, and softer,

the wind and the powdery glass like dandelion white parachutes adrift through the opening, through the window and down, angled from the hall mirror and pulled inward to the living room, falling soft, clumsily, full-bodied onto the hardwood floor. He has returned to the space he keeps. It is dark. The light's reflection shines white in the night of the front window, the outline complete, precise. He sleeps. Outside, he hears the loud confidence of the engine, the steel wheels of the cars at high speed along the rails. In the early morning the old woman puts a hand on his shoulder. The touch awakens him. Yes, he thinks, I will leave this place.

The next day he rises, moves south and west to Bozeman. No jobs, but big, he gets work in a feed store. He passes a placement exam and enrolls in the agricultural college in Bozeman. He rides bulls in every rodeo he can find. Nearly every Saturday night he fights in bars. He doesn't drink. He seeks only the concave feel of facial structure, the slippery skin of cheekbones, the line of a man's nose, the loose pendulum of the jawbone and the cool sockets of the eyes. He likes these things, the sound they make as they give way, the sound of cartilage and the way the skin slits open before the blood begins, the white-hard glisten of bone, the sound of the face when it breaks. But he hates himself that he likes it.

Still he returns. In the half-dark of the bar in the basement of the Wellington Hotel outside White Sulphur he opens the curve of a man's head on the corner of a table. A small mob gathers seeking revenge, the man's brothers, the man's friends. He throws them back and puts out the teeth from the mouth of one. He breaks the elbow of another. You'll leave here dead, he says, and the group recedes, the power in him vital and full and he walks from the open door alone into darkness until he sits off distant, wrapping his knees in his arms, weeping.

He seeks to turn himself and he turns. He fights less. He

wanders more, dirt streets of rodeo towns when the day is done, the lit roads of Bozeman in the night after his reading. It is the sound of gravel beneath his boots he seeks, a multitude of small stones forming a silver path under the moon and sky, leading nowhere. He graduates college, barely passing, a first in agribusiness, a second in accounting, Depression on, jobs scarce. He builds roads, digs ditches, dams, gets on at Fort Peck, his home a hillside cutout, tarp angled over woodstove, single three-leg stool, small lamp of oil, he smells the earth, he sleeps on dirt. North still but jobless, he waits overnight in a line of one hundred men. The head man sees his size. He gets on as a workman with the railroad. He'll earn some money, buy himself some land. Perhaps buy back the land they lost. Plant a hedge of wild rose, he thinks, for his mother. He is six feet nine inches tall and weighs over three hundred pounds. He works the Empire Builder, the interstate rail from east to west. He works with muscle and grit. He shovels coal. He keeps his own peace.

Alone in the late push across the borderlands they ride the Hi-Line of Montana and he stops for a moment and rests his hands on the heel of the shovel, rests his chin on his hands. He feels the locomotive spending its light toward the oncoming darkness, toward the tiny crossings with unknown names, the towns of eight or ten people. He feels the wide wind, sees the stars in their opaque immensity. He hears the long-nosed scream of the train, bent in the night, and he pauses and considers how fully the night falls, how easily the light gives way, then he returns to his work.

Late he lies himself down in his sleeping berth. He stinks of smoke and oil, the sweating film of his body envelops him and he falls toward sleep as one who has come from the earth, who has molded it with his hands, who has returned again. In his place in the dark, always he hears his mother. Mind your schooling, she says. It is after dinner. She lays him down. He is a child sleeping, and in the silence between night and dawn, waking him she speaks her elegant words, presses her cheek to his small cheek, whispers, Awake, awake, O Zion, clothe yourself in strength. Put on your garments of splendor. She smooths his eyebrows with a forefinger. You can get up now, she says. She touches his face with her hand.

It is not yet dawn. He lies on his side, sees on the hard shelf before his eyes the ivory hair comb bright as bone. He takes the comb in the curve of his hand. He lies still. He puts the comb to his lips in the transparent light. He breathes his deep and holy breath. He remembers the clean smell of her hair. Along the spine of the comb he moves his index finger, then he eyes his finger for a moment, coal and dirt deep set in the whorls. He draws his hand to his mouth and licks the tip of his finger. The sun has broken the far line of the world. His tongue tastes of light.

He works the train and travels to places he has not yet known, where day is buoyant and darkness gone, and when death comes seeking like the hand of an enemy he gives himself over, for it is death he desires, and death he welcomes, and the spirit of his good body is a vessel borne to the eternal.

2

HE IS BORN INTO THIS WORLD, he is named. He is made of
dirt and fighting and the grace of his mother's words. He is one.
He is caught in the mass of many. The earth bends beneath him
and he listens to the whistle of the train, the notes like a voice of
reason in the early dark that wakens him and returns him, takes
him weary back to the loaded pull of the cars, the sound of the
push and the steel of the tracks.

He rises. He begins again.

The older men on the line call him Middie because they've
heard talk of him breaking the back of a bull that wouldn't carry
his weight. It was at a rodeo he entered when he was nineteen, up
in Glendive. The bull was old and skinny, put in by a local farmer
as a joke. The bull didn't show enough verve, so the boy bucked
the animal himself.

Bent its middle like a bow, the vet said. Sprung its spine.

The bull had to be put down. The boy had both hated and
delighted in this, delighted in undoing the farmer's intention, hated that the animal was hard done by. The railroaders
laugh their heads off and Middie has to listen to them nearly
every stop. They sit behind their counters at each station chewing the fat with Prifflach the conductor as they tell and retell
what they've heard. Middie doesn't like them. When they speak
they look through him, just as Prifflach does. He is nothing to
them. He lets them think they own him. He has a job, he bides
his time. The railroad furthers the chasm between father and
mother. Something lower down is revealed, something more
sedentary and rooted even than the earth that had opened and
closed, closing over him the darker image of his father alongside
the subtle light of his mother, the stiff shock of his father's hair
under snow, the gray, grainy look of his mother's teeth long after
the last exhalation, after he'd found her in her bed.

Riding the Hi-Line he is mostly unseen by the passengers as

he hauls freight and works coal. But a change in duty comes, a change he doesn't welcome. He'll provide muscle for the boss-man, the conductor, Ed Prifflach. Three times tossing drunks to local sheriffs at the next stop, twice tracking rich old lady no-shows still wandering after the all aboard. Then the real trouble begins. Just past Wolf Point, when the first theft is discovered, Middie is put in charge of public calm. He keeps to the plan and follows Prifflach's words though it is distasteful to him, though he begins to feel in the eyes of others he is becoming the con-ductor's efficacy, an outline of Prifflach's power, a bigger, more mobile expression.

Things aren't what they seem, Middie thinks. Danger, for reasons a man doesn't comprehend. On his first trip east a work-man at the roundhouse in St. Paul threw himself between the cars of an outgoing train. When Middie got word he went to see. The man was severed in two at the chest. Middie isn't afraid to die, and when he dies he wants it to be hard and without any hope of return, as physical as rock so he can feel the skin give, the bones in the cavernous weight of his body broken, and blood like a river moving from the center of him, pooling out and away and down into the earth, to the soil that receives him and sets him free.

In the first compartment Prifflach leans toward him, non-chalant in body in order to avoid alarm even as he yells at him to surmount the noise. First seat, worst position, thinks Middie, while Prifflach sets the course with regard to the thief. Get some leads, he says. Prifflach's face is wolflike, a man with large but-tocks, hairy arms and hands. Middie dislikes him, his sunken eyes, the haughty tenor of his voice. Happening nearly every stop now, Prifflach says. Bad for business. Under a long, narrow nose his mouth tightens. The line ain't gonna like it, guaranteed. Give me the tally.

Five people, says Middie.

Tally his take, says Prifflach.

Middie uses a small piece of paper, a gnawed pencil. Near four hundred dollars, he says, four hundred ten to be precise. His face feels colorless, his body breathes in and out.

Get going, Middie, Prifflach says.

Middie stares at the double doors with their elongated rect-angular glass, two top squares open for the heat. Prifflach said he'd picked him because Middie had thighs like cottonwoods and thick arms.

Look alive, Middie.

He hears the words, notes Prifflach's face. Wet lines in a wax head. Then he looks at the people.

A weight of soot covers everyone. Their eyes are swollen and bloodshot. They have stiff red necks. On their laps they hold children and bags, gripping them as if to ward off death. Middie peers at the faces, and farther back, through more doors at the end of the car, more elongated squares of glass into the second car where expressions breathe the same contempt, the shadow of a shadow, the same self-preservation, the same undignified desire. They are on the upswing through great carved moun-tains and though Middie has worked the round trip St. Paul to Spokane five times, he still feels unlanded here, awkward under the long slow ascent of the train, the sheer drop of landscape, of trees and earth, and way down, the thin, flat line of the river.

Side windows remain mostly shut, frozen in place by the inter-lock of the moisture inside and the frigid temperature of early winter outside. The air in the compartments, especially those closest to the heat of the locomotive, is heavy, thick to the lungs, and lined with body odor.

Middie has succeeded, through a forceful combination of the billy club Prifflach issued him and a jackknife he carries, in slightly opening the casement adjoining his seat. Air slides through the sliver of space he's created and Middie can feel it, even if the chug of the train taints it all, he feels the clean blade of pine, the rich

taste of high mountains, the snicker of winter, windy and sublimi-
nal. He feels Bearhat Mountain and Gunsight out there, the draw
of Going to the Sun Road lining the opposite side of the valley,
spare of people now, the park locked in the grip of September,
closed to visitors but for the oil and punch of the train, and the
Blackfeet nation in the expanse below the great rocks.

Looking out he feels the calling an eagle might feel in the drafts
over the backbone of the continent, that something of light and
stone and water, perhaps fire, has created him and breathed life
through the opening of his lips, and there is a violence in that, he
thinks, and a tenderness, and he sees as if with the eyes of a child
the wings of the eagle thrown wide over the body of the beloved,
the scream of the bird in the highborne wind.

YET A DARK PALL covers Middie's eyes; he stares at everyone sus-
piciously. When Prifflach rises, Middie follows. They walk a few
steps and sit down again in another couplet of chairs, aimed back
down the corridor, to the next car, and the next. People are seen in
a long line, from compartment to compartment, bumped by the
small clicks and turns of the train, jilted forward, hitched to the
side, bumped back. The people say nothing. They clutch their bags.

The scenario sickens him. Too many people. Too public. If he
was alone, or in the dark of barrooms, he'd feel clear, free to do as
he wished, but here the fray of his mind annoys him. He brushes
the tips of his fingers over his left shirt pocket, the cloth there
housing his mother's comb, he feels the form of it, the tines like
a small alien hand. He's already checked them all three times
by order of Prifflach. Once each after the last three stops: Wolf
Point, Glasgow, Malta. The first time, he apologized, comforting
an older woman on her way to see her son in Spokane. Prifflach
had sent a wire out at Glasgow, inquiring what to do. The second check more of the same, this time soothing the worry of a
young woman off to the state agricultural school in Pullman.

Prifflach called it coincidence—two different burglars, two different towns, a little over three hundred dollars missing. But
after the third stop, at Malta, when an elderly man was found
dead, his head askew, a small well of blood in his right ear, the
rumors poisoned every compartment.

He had money, said the help in the dining car. Paid for his
meals in crisp new bills. But when Middie checked the body,
Prifflach looking over his shoulder, there was nothing, no money,
not even any silver. Middie felt the minds of the people beginning to hum and move and he sensed the interior of Prifflach,
angry as if cornered, pushing him to take action. Middie hated
it, but the line chose him, and he was big.

On the first check no one resisted; everyone simply wanted
the thief caught. Even the second check people remained po-
lite, just grimaced some while Middie displaced their bags and
Prifflach went through them. Middie had to pat the people
down, search their coats, their clothing, have them empty each
of their pockets. It took far longer than he wished, but mostly
the people smiled and tried to be helpful. On the third round
the death had changed things. The women whispered and
shrank back from him. The body itself, alone in a sleeping car
until the next stop, was like an imprint of the predator among
them. Middie felt the tension of it, the people's thoughts in
fearful accord, like a dark vein of cloud swept into the bank of
mountains, collecting, preparing.

Prifflach declared all must hand over their weapons and
named Middie the one to gather them. The men glared at
Middie as Prifflach rifled their bags. Some were openly angry.
Many, he thought, suspected him, or Prifflach. Only a few gave
up their arms, and unwillingly, a cluster of pistols, four Colts,
two Derringers, along with one rifle. Other men lied, though
Middie felt their weapons, in a bootleg or under the arm, the
stock of a gun, the handle of a knife. He decided not to press

and Prifflach silently colluded, the potential threat subduing the
conductor's zeal. What Middie retrieved he stored in the engi-
neer's cab. Returning, he walked the aisles and felt weary. People
don't like being pushed.

The next stop, Havre, town of locked-in winters, town of
bars. At last, the removal of the dead man, to be shipped back to
Chicago. Not dusk or dawn, but day, not night as Middie would
hope, nor the color of night. The body is well blanketed, taken
off from the back of the train. Middie carries it across the platform and it feels light to him, almost birdlike in his arms. He
turns his back to shield the view. Prifflach holds the door for
him and as Middie enters the station he catches over Prifflach's
shoulder the faces of passengers in the fourth car, most of them
pale and dumb-looking, not meeting his eye. But one, an Indian
man he'd noticed on his passenger checks, a crossbreed, looks
right at him. He remembers seeing him board the train in Wolf
Point. The Indian's eyes are black from where Middie stands. He
imagines round irises among the slanted whites; it reminds him
of how people had stared at this man during the checks, a few
uttering quiet threats while the man stared back at them as if
taunting them to put meaning to their words. Despite the fact
that the Indian was well dressed, Middie had had to quiet the
car twice as they searched him.

Inside the station Middie hears Prifflach tell the attendant
the death is nothing. Old man died in his sleep, Prifflach says.
Line informed the family; they'll meet the body in St. Paul. The
attendant is a potbellied bald man, chewing snuice. Prifflach or-
ders Middie back to the train to watch the passengers. No sheriff, thinks Middie. Line saving its own skin. Close-mouthed, he
looks at Prifflach, but the conductor waves him on and Middie
does as he is told.

He sits on the train, puts his head in his hands, runs them
through his hair, then disembarks, rounds the platform and

crosses the dirt street. Between two buildings, the wind, low to
the ground and fast from the north, bends a cluster of three
bitterroot blooms. A kind of gesture, he thinks, and kneels to
behold them, the bright stamens like small cathedrals, shaken
not destroyed.

He approaches the front door of the Stockman Bar. Door
painted black, oiled hinges, inside a dim small room and three
tables, dark marble counter with five stools, the place is clean,
a lone bartender wipes things down. Help you? he says. No,
Middie answers, the murmur of his voice barely audible. He
needs a chair to sit in, a space to calm his mind. The bartender
spits in a tin cup on the counter. You don't drink, you don't
stay, he says. Middie feels things shutting down, his insides are
heavy and tight, the center of him like an eclipse that obscures
the light, three quick steps to the barman and one fist that
rides the force of hip and shoulder, the man laid cold on the
hardwood floor. Not dead, but still, and flat-backed. Middie,
seated in the chair he desires, watches the blood curl from a
three-inch line over the man's eye, elliptic down his face to his
neck, to the floor. Orbital bone still sound, eyes rolled back
in the head, the man is motionless as Middie considers him.
Should've been Prifflach, he says aloud. But saying it Middie
feels broken. He can't go back. His eyes are grave, dark as his father's. Darkness covers the earth and deep darkness its people.
It is a darkness he feels he cannot undo. But he must. He will.
Prifflach comes cursing, and Middie walks in the conductor's
shadow, back to the train, the people.

Three quick halts at Shelby, Cutbank, and Browning. East
Glacier next, the station at the park's east entrance, the one
with the Blackfeet Agency greeting in which three Indians wait
on the small gray platform in full regalia. An elder in full eagle-
feather headdress gives out cigars. Two women in white deerskin
dresses sell beadwork. Only a handful of white passengers gawk

this time, not all as is customary. Most remain subdued, brooding, sitting in their seats. Then on the track past East Glacier, as the train climbs the high boundary toward the west side of the park and the depot at Belton, two more reports of impropriety, two more thefts, lesser, but significant, one of sixty dollars, the other forty. Not counting the unknown amount stolen from the dead man, the total, as Middie said, had reached four hundred and ten.

Middie loathes the thought of checking bags again. He thinks the people, all of them, close and far, dislike him. Some of the faces are full of disdain.

So? says Prifflach.

Yes? says Middie.

So start another check, says Prifflach. He speaks like a crow, thinks Middie. He watches Prifflach pull a small piece of paper from his vest pocket, the wire retrieved from the Havre station in answer to his plea at Glasgow. Prifflach turns the paper to Middie, shows these words: keep quiet—no police—security man finds thief—or loses job.

No good, says Middie, awkward, aloud, using a tone he'd seen his mother use to calm his father. Look at them, Middie says, motioning with his eyes to the people around him.

Prifflach turns on him, sharp-faced, and what he says makes Middie desire to kill him. It's your own good, boy. Line's takin' you out if you don't get it done. Move.

Middie sees it coming, and he wishes against it, but he knows no other alternative. All that college. Up against the wall with book learning, and nothing now for real life. Heavy shouldered, he rises from his seat. He begins again.

Pardon me, may I see your bag? and, Pardon, sir, I have to look through your personal effects. The words are graceful in Middie's mind, his mind electric, his body like a fine-tuned instrument.

BUT PEOPLE ARE NOW OPENLY HOSTILE. A woman in the
first car, one in the second, and one in the third make a scene and
won't unhand their bags. He pulls the bags from the first two, and
lets Prifflach search the contents while he quickly pats the people
down and pushes his fingers in their coat pockets. When he approaches the third woman she claws a bright hole in his cheek.
His mind thinks terrible things. Ugly, he tells himself. Ugly. Has
to be done, though. Other passengers help him do it too, they
hold the woman back while he searches her and while Prifflach
gives the bag a thorough inspection. Idiots, Middie thinks, all
of them, and me with them. They see it too, the people. They
all admit inwardly the logic is imprecise, but better than doing
nothing. Check everyone or it's no use. Futile, Middie thinks,
a man can hide money anywhere. When he returns the third
woman's bag she curses him. Then she looks him in the face,
says God curse you, and turns her back.

Middie can't remember ever having heard a woman speak like
that. He walks from the third car toward the fourth, opens the
double doors at the end of the compartment, closes the doors
behind. He stands on the deck, hears the raw howl of the train,
the wind. Something will happen now. To his left a wall of wet
granite undulates, hard and dark, blurred by the train speed. He
looks up and sees the great face of it arching, reaching up and out,
thousands of feet of rock, jagged and pinnacled at the top, swept
up and out over the roof of the train. Beyond this, the gray sky is
low and thick. The look of it gives him vertigo and he turns his
head down and grips the handrail. He sees his worn boots on the
grated steel. His mother, he thinks, he can't remember her face.

To his right he can feel the valley out there, spread wide in a
pattern of darks and lighter darks, filled from above by the distant pull of fog and rain. The downpour falls in wide diagonal
sheets, descending into massive rock blacks and rock grays far on
the other side of the valley. Among the bases of the mountains,

forests are spread like cloaks. The water runs hard from the runoff of the storm and everything converges to a river colored black as the curve of a gun barrel. The river is the middle fork of the Flathead, past the summit of Marias Pass and past the great trestle of Two Medicine Bridge. They've crested the Great Divide and the train's muscle pumps faster now, louder on the down westward grade. The river runs due west from here, seeming to bury itself into the wide forested skirt of a solitary mass of land. The flat-topped tower of the mass is obscured, mostly covered over by wet fog, but visible in its singularity and the ominous feel of something hidden in darkness, something entirely individual, devoid of any other, accountable to neither sky nor storm. At the mountain's height a black ridge is barely detectable. The hulk of the land feels gargantuan. Is it Grinnell Point or Reynolds Mountain, Cleveland or Apikuni? He can't make it out.

Here in Middie's reverie, muffled shouts are heard, faint like the far-off cry of a cat. He looks up to the doors of the fourth car, the final passenger car. Slender windows frame what he sees and suddenly the words, though disembodied, come clean. I've got him! yells a fatty-faced man, sealed up there in the box of the car. I've got the mother-hatin' rat.

Middie leaps forward, opening the fourth car, shouting, Stop! Wait! About midway up the car the fatty-faced man, and now four others, have thrown a man to the floor in the aisle. The man wears a brown tweed suit, he makes a vigorous struggle with his assailants.

It's him! cries the fat one. We caught him red-handed.

To avoid the wild flail, passengers press back against the walls. Women push their children in behind them, children with wide eyes, lit with fear.

Let go, says Middie, staring at the fat man, and the men heed his word quickly and without complaint. Middie is struck by the fear men harbor, larger than a child's, and he recognizes suddenly the pure sway he holds, because he is big, over people, over men.

The captive stands in the aisle and brushes wrinkles from his suit, his hair flung forward, black and thick over his face. Dark-eyed. The Indian, thinks Middie, as he draws nearer.

When the man pushes his hair back, the bones of his face appear chiseled in stone, the skin a thin casing for all the intrepid want in him. Thin as a sheet of newsprint, Middie thinks, ready to tear open, ready for it all to break out. The man tucks in his shirt and realigns his belt. He straightens his vest, then the lapels of his jacket, visibly pulling the tension back in and down, breathing. He is silent. He views his captors with contempt, each one.

Middie pictures his firm step and upright gait when he first walked the aisle and positioned his bags. Assiniboine-Sioux he'd thought. Wolf Point. But after pulling his bag and questioning him four times he'd found him to be a Blackfeet-white cross, Blood in fact, a Blackfeet subtribe (and Irish on the other side, he'd said, one clan or another). He was on his way to his family's home south of West Glacier after a "work-related" trip to Wolf Point. Middie had checked him once more than all the rest. The man said he taught at the college in Missoula. In education, he said. They locked eyes when Middie carried the dead man at Havre, but Middie had dismissed it and other than the agitation of the crowd during the checks, an agitation Middie felt always accompanied whites and Indians, he had found nothing unusual. The man carried no weapon.

What is it? Middie asks the man with the fat head.

A short man, a man with slick hair, one of the others who had held the accused, speaks up vehemently. This man—he points in the Indian's face—this man has been lying! He's the one. He took all the money.

Slow, says Middie. Say what you know.

I have not lied, says the prisoner.

Shut up! the slick man yells.

Middie puts a forearm to the slick man's chest. Settle yourself, he says. Sit down.

The slick man obeys, whispering something, glaring. He's
lying, he says. Hiding something.

How do you know?

Check his side, see for yourself. He's had his hand there in his
jacket from the start.

The fat man butts in, edging with rage, He won't show us
what he's got in there.

Is it true, sir? asks Middie, heightening his politeness. Is there
something hidden in your waistcoat?

Yes, he states, looking into Middie's face, but that makes me
neither a liar nor guilty of the offense in question.

We will check it, sir, Middie replies, but he feels aggravated.
He doesn't like the uppity tone the Indian has used. What have
you concealed? Middie asks.

My money belt, says the man.

MIDDIE HARDENS HIS LOOK. His hands sweat. He wipes
them on his pant legs as he stares at the man. Probably had it
on his waistline, Middie thinks, concealed under the clothing,
probably thin as birch bark. He remembers Prifflach muttering
under his breath at the Indian as he checked the man's bag,
a small cylindrical briefcase made of beaten brown leather,
sealed at the top by a thin zipper that ran between two worn
handles, the word MONTANA inscribed on the side. Mostly papers in the bag.

You have searched my briefcase and my wallet, says the man,
and me once more than the others. I saw no need for you to
search my money belt. And if I had shown you my belt, would
that not become a target for the robber if he were present in this
compartment during the search?

Don't listen to him, the slick man says in a wet voice, he's slippery.

The crowd murmurs uneasily. Middie notes that outside, the fog has pressed in. Nothing of the valley can be seen, and nothing of the sky. The mountains will be laid low, Middie thinks. He hears the words soft and articulate in his mother's voice. Outside is the featureless gray of a massive fog bank, and behind it a feeling of the bulk of the land.

Check his belt, the fat face says.

Then the crowd begins. See what he's got, says a red-haired woman, the fat man's wife by the look of it, the small eyes, the clutching, heavy draw of the cheeks about the jowls. She says the words quietly but they are enough to hasten a flood. Do it now, hears Middie. Make him hand it over, Take it from him, Pull up his shirt, Take it—all from the onlookers, all at once, and from somewhere low and small back behind Middie, the quiet words, Cut his throat.

The conductor arrives and Middie exhales and feels his body go slack; he stares outside. The gray-black of the storm leaks moisture on the windows. The moisture gathers and pulls lines sideways along the windows, minuscule lines in narrow groupings of hundreds and wide bars of thousands, rivulets and the brothers of rivulets, and within them the broad hordes of their children, their offspring, all pulled back along the glass to the end of the train, to the end of seeing.

You will have him hand over that money belt directly, says Prifflach, his nose leading, his face pinched, set like clay. Pressure builds in the bodycage of Middie, a pressure that pushes out against his skin. Middie reaches and grabs the accused man's wrist, gripping the flesh with frozen fingers, red-white fingers latching on.

To Middie's relief the man responds. With one arm in Middie's grip, the man uses his free hand to untuck the front of his shirt. He slides the money belt to a point above his waist, and undoes the small metal clasps that hold the belt in place. His fingers so meticulous, thinks Middie, so dexterous and sure. Eyes as clear as the sky before they reached Glacier, cold and steely-black. Middie looks again to the window. His own reflection is not unlike the gray outside, and behind it the unpeopled weight of land, the emptiness. He notes he has left his billy club in the last compartment, on the floor near a seat where he'd checked a man's ankles, his socks. Middie's fists feel big, hard as stones. He doesn't need it, he tells himself.

Give up the belt, Prifflach says, though already the man is pulling the belt free.

He holds it out to the conductor. Nothing out of the ordinary, he says. I'm simply a man carrying my own money. His hair is still bent, his shirt poorly tucked. He does not look away from his accusers.

At once, the fat man and his wife shout something unintelligible.

We'll see, says the conductor, interpreting their words. We'll see if it's his money. At the corners of Prifflach's mouth the skin twitches. Prifflach takes the money belt and hands it to the slick man. Count it up, he says, watching the Indian's face.

The slick man thumbs the money once, finding an unfortunate combination of bigger and smaller bills. How much is there? asks the conductor. The slick man counts again, slowly. Five hundred ten dollars, he says. Exactly one hundred more than the amount stolen. Middie knows a desire has gripped them, and that they all, silently, hastily, have calculated the old dead man's loss at a clean one hundred. Middie has done the same.

I could have told you that, says the accused.

Prifflach tells the man to shut up, then says, A hundred dollars more than the total. He folds the money belt in half, and half again; I'll take that, he says, placing it in the chest pocket of his coat.

It comes clear to Middie now, the look of the onlookers, the way of their eyes and their bodies, how they've all torn loose inside, all come unspun. He remembers what he'd read in a pamphlet at the West Glacier station a month ago. Something of a hidden passage west, close to the headwaters of the Marias, a high mountain pass that according to Indian belief was steeped in the spirit world, inhabited by a dark presence. Decades back, when the line first wanted to chart its track through here, no Indian would take a white man through. Death inhabited the place.

Middie sees the demeanor of the Blackfeet man change. The man's face loses expression, his body pulls inward. In the space between them Middie senses the man gathering himself. A surge is felt, up through the flesh of the Indian's forearm. Middie tightens his grip.

The crowd moves. Suspected him back in Glasgow, a stout man pipes up. I should have known, says another, and from the slick man, He ain't gettin' outta here. Low again, deep back in the crowd, a voice says, Slit his throat.

The movement begins in words and rustling, then leaps upward like a mighty wave that breaks upon the people and the man all at once. The Blackfeet man jerks free and jumps the chair back next to him, seeking to flank the men and escape from the rear of the compartment. The men scramble after him, Prifflach leading, the others following, all of them livid with hate.

Middie vaults a set of chairs and lands on the Blackfeet man, slamming him bodily against the sidewall of the car. The man rights himself and spits in Middie's face and Middie, fueled now, lifts him and encircles the Indian's neck in the crook of his left arm, positioning him. He props him up, left hand on the man's shoulder as he holds him. Then he levels a blow with the right that bounces the Blackfeet man's head off the near window, flings his hair like a horsetail, and leaves a grotesque indentation where the cheekbone has caved in. Four other men, along with Middie, jerk the prisoner from the wall, shake him hand over fist to the aisleway. They surround him, and proceed to drag him toward the back of the car. The shoving lurches the Indian forward and makes his neck look thin, snaps his head back, throws his eyes to the ceiling.

What are you doing? he cries out, I'm innocent, and straining from the hands that grasp at his upper body he turns his face to the window, to the gray valley beyond, and says, I have a wife. I have a child.

With shocking swiftness the Indian throws his forearms out and lunges forward with his head in order to strike someone. But now his flailings are as nothing to the weight of the accusers: there are many men now, their arms entangled in his limbs, controlling him easily. They punch him in the back, and in the back of the head. Keep your head down! they say; You'll lose your teeth in a second. The group is packed in, forming a tight untidy ball in the aisleway and among the spaces between the seats. A thick odor is in the air.

The prisoner's head is near the floor. Reaching for the Indian's waist, Middie sees a look of resignation, a look of light among the features of his face. The man stares at Middie and whispers something Middie cannot hear or understand.

Amidst the tumult a smaller voice says, Wait! It comes from behind Middie, up near the front of the car. Turning, looking up and back through the moving heads, back behind the bending, pressing torsos, Middie sees the source of the voice, a small man, adolescent in appearance, thin-boned in a simple two-piece suit. The man has fine, blond hair and oval wire-rimmed glasses.

Wait! the man says, I know him.

A large man at the back of the mob turns to the boyish man and says, You shut up.

The small man's face goes red, he shrinks back to his seat. Middie sees this and turns back to the mob. The people are grabbing the Blackfeet man's clothing in their hands and shaking his body like a child's doll. Men are emerging from their seats, running the aisles like ants, joining the mob. The man's limbs appear loose in the torque of the crowd. The arms move as if boneless, the elbows seem disconnected from the shoulders.

From his vantage Middie turns and sees the little man with his head down now as the people swirl toward the rear of the car, down to the doors they have already pulled back and the opening tilted like a black mouth from which the wind screams. Middie hears the accused grunting, cursing. The little man rises and walks directly to the rear guard of the mob. Unable to get through he sidesteps the knot of people. He climbs over three or four seats as he repositions women and children. He travels awkwardly but insistent, like a leggy insect, toward the back of the compartment, toward the opening and the landing beyond. He goes unrecognized by all but Middie and when he reaches the far wall of the car, he stops, and stares. The prisoner is held about the neck by the thick hands of Prifflach, clinched about the waist by Middie and on both sides by bold, angry men.

The small man positions himself, mounting the arms of the last two aislechairs so that he stands directly before the mob. He straddles the aisle, the land a blur in the open doorway behind him, around him the live wind a strange unholy combustion. He draws his fists to his sides, billows his chest as he gathers air, and screams, Stop! A wild scream, high and sharp like the bark of a dog.

The little man's effort creates a brief moment of quiet in which the people stand gaping at him. Seizing this, he strings his words rapidly. I know him. I spoke with him when he got on in Wolf Point. He has a three-year-old daughter. He has a wife. He has a good mother, a father. He will be dropped off at the stop on the far side of Glacier where they are waiting for him. He will return with them by car to the Mission Range.

Shut up, says the fat man.

I won't, says the small man. He told me precisely.

He lied, says the slick man.

Let me speak, the small man pleads. He touches his hand to his face, a gesture both elegant and tremulous.

We won't, the mob responds, and in their movement and in the pronounced gather of their voices the prisoner is lifted by the neck and shoved forward toward the door.

Out of the way! someone yells, and Middie watches as the small man takes a blow to the side of the head, a shot of tremendous force that lifts him light as goosedown, unburdened in flight to where his body hits the wall near the floor of the car and he lies crumpled, his face lolling to one side. Thickly now the small man says, He told me precisely. His words are overrun but he continues. He told me precisely, in Wolf Point. Before all of this, he had five hundred ten dollars of earnings. He meant to do what he and his wife dreamed. Middie's fists are bound up in the clothing of the Blackfeet man, his forearms are bone to bone with the man's ribs. The little man is speaking, He meant to buy land, off the reservation. The voice seems small, down between the chairs, He meant to build a home.

The opening through which they pass is wide, the small man's body a bit of detritus they have cast aside, the landing now beneath their feet solid and whole, like a long-awaited rest. Middie hears the velocity of wind and steel as he flows with the crowd to the brink. He feels the rush, like the expectancy of power in a bull's back when the gate springs wide, like the sound of a man's jaw when it breaks loose.

Also he feels sorrow; he wants to cry or cry out. He wants to reach for the ivory hair comb but a weight of bodies presses him from behind and his hands are needed to control the captive. He feels the indent of the guardrail firmly on his thigh. He hears the small man's voice, back behind him. He told me at Wolf Point— precisely five hundred ten dollars. Five hundred ten.

The landing is narrow, the people many, and they are knotted and pushed forward by a score more, angry men running from other cars, clogging the aisle to get to the man. Those at the front grab the railing, the steel overhead bars, they grab each other, the Indian, the enemy. Noise surrounds them, the train's cry, the wide burn of descent, the people's yells high and sharp above every-thing, shrill as if from the mouths of predatory birds. The Indian's suitcoat and vest are gone. His slim torso looks clean in his worried shirt, a V-shaped torso, trim and strong. In the press of it Middie is hot. Oxlike, he feels the burden of everyone, borne at once in him, and he bends and grabs the man's leg. Other men do the same, there are plenty of hands now. He wants to hold the man fast but instead the crowd shoves the man aloft. They tip him upside down and clutch his ankles as they remove his shoes. They tear off his shirt, then his ribbed undershirt. They throw the shoes down among the tracks. The clothing they throw out into the wind where it whisks away and falls, rolling and descending like white leaves deep into the fog of the valley.

From here the man is lowered between the cars. He becomes silent. Below the captive, Middie sees the silvery gleam of the tracks, parallel lines in the black blur of the ties, the lines bend-ing almost imperceptibly at times, silver but glinting dull like teeth. With his elbows he tries to hold the people back. He feels the oncoming force of the crowd behind him, the jealousy, the desire. A woman's voice is heard, a voice he knows but does not recognize. He bows his back and groans, trying to draw the man forth. The words are like a song, simple and beautiful in his mind: Put on your garments of splendor. He smells the oil of the train, the heat, the wet rock of the mountain.

He sets his jaw and strains, he would pull the people and the man and the whole world to the mercy of his will; he gains no ground.

In the gusts of wind, the mob squints their eyes. Leaning for-ward, their hair is blown back, it swirls some, blows back again.

The speed of the train and the noise of the tracks, the scent of high sage and jack pine, the fogged void of gray as wide and deep as an ocean, but foremost the wind, rushes up against the mob creating an almost still-life movement into which they carry the man. Then the wind dies. The river of people flowing from the compartment bottlenecks in the doorway. Bodies from the choked opening to the guardrail twist and writhe and a vast shouting commences. Middie says No! This must stop! He grips the Blackfeet man's belt with both fists and pulls him upward. His big body is a countermovement against the rise of all around him, but angry yells issue from wide red mouths and the mob grows to an impossible mass that pushes and swells, and breaks free in a sudden gush. Middie finds himself with the Indian airborne, cast into the gulf without foot or handhold, he has lost everything, and falling he sees a shaft of blue high in the gray above him and he is surprised at how light he feels, and how time has slowed to nothing. He reaches back, seeking a purchase he will not find, and in the singular sweep of his arm he takes people unaware—Prifflach, the fat man, his wife, the slick man—they all fly from the edge, effortless in the push of the mob, unstrung bodies and tight faces, over the lip of the guardrail and down between the cars, down to the tracks, the wheels, the black pump of the smoking engine, the yell of the machine.

—for my grandmother, whom we call the Great One

THREE FROM MONTANA

"You ever see a house burning up in the night . . ."
—Annie Proulx

I. THE LAND

NO HISTORY GOES on unheard, no atrocity—the shootings and the sex crimes, the monstrosities, the mayhems that inhabit the ranch towns and small cities: Cohagen of eight people, Miles City of ten thousand, Plenty Coups more than one hundred, Bozeman tens of thousands. In Montana, skies tilt from a wooden porch all the way to the horizon line, and nothing keeps back the dawn. Cars from the reservations, dirty white trucks, yellow buses packing in hundreds, carting fans to basketball games in midwinter, the sons of trappers and the daughters of sheep shearers, the blood of a child in the trunk of an Eldorado, white crosses in twos or fives at the bends of this two-lane mountain are nearly transparent in the backlight. Everyone who has ever come here, remains. The land and the vault of sky are everything and people so insignificant they are struck by the idea that God doesn't owe them anything.

They are together in the deep high country, his father, his

brother, himself. Much older than they were. All three grown now, each of them men. Shale and Weston brothers. Edwin their father. They are still together, a lie Shale tells himself, knowing Weston flew from the edge of Beargrass Mountain and died in a car crash at twenty-two. But he carries Weston with him, knows he always will, and yes, knows his father carries him too. A thick layer of cloud surrounds the peak up high to their right, rounded, massive shoulder, forested at the base beneath the cloud cover, treeless and rocky at the top where it breaks free crowned in dawn's light. Birds fly in the drafts, gold dark eagles. To the south the cloud bank thins and open sky reaches from the slight promontory where they stand, holding their arms, looking out, down the draw of scrub pine and mottled veins of sage, blown timothy grass bent to the ground and everything converging along the silver-blue of the big river. Out from there the sweep of the valley, the four directions, the compass rose, and far to the south a landmass like the broad back of a giant sleeper. The air comes from the north, chill and fast from the great gap of Canada down the channel from Glacier over the western mid-Montana plains to the mountains again, the line that unites the Beartooths, the Bridgers, the Spanish Peaks, and blind northeast behind them the Crazies. The bold land—cerulean forms of three plateaus, the one high bulk of mountain with gold swept among the blue, and in the shadowed valley the brown and tan of earth and grasses bound to the mercury of river water, boulders like crumbled towers, and sky bigger, flung out more bold than all—the land takes them and holds them. The land delivers them. Shale contemplates what he sees. God didn't owe us anything, he thinks, but he gave his most beloved.

II. THE FIRST DEFINITION OF PRETTY

Shale was nine years old. Weston eleven. They'd been summoned to the relic zone, their parents' bedroom, a place the boys walked through quietly so as not to disturb anything. They'd been there so rarely the room fascinated them. A mirror plate trimmed in silver lay flat on the dark wood bureau, set with Mother's rings and lead crystal vials of perfume. The boys sat on the end of the bed, their feet hanging toward the floor. They sat on a blue flowered bedspread that was military sharp, pillows encased and tucked with a hard feminine hand. It was the femininity of it, the absence of the masculine that surprised and hushed them because they considered the great power he had over her, and they felt deeply the facade of this room, the fear that held her here, her sanctuary in the evenings and into night when he manned the living room watching TV, or when his presence downtown with alcohol and whatever he did when he was gone became a silence in the home that was physical. Her mind ran circles while she lay off to one side in the bed under the tight curve of clean sheets and straight coverlet; she heard the sound of her boys breathing, sleeping down the hall. At night, they'd heard her weep so many times they had no words.

They sat there, Shale and his older brother, at the edge of the bed, in the elegant feel of that place, in the gold light of the afternoon. They had never met in their mother and father's bedroom. They met here today. Their father had never cried in their presence.

He was a big man, six feet four, nearly 250 pounds. He held his hands together, pressed them to his forehead, moved them away. His face was bent, twisting at the mouth and the eyes. The body was bent too, inward with shoulders rounded, chest caved in. His arms surrounded the cavity he created. His hands worked in the middle, folded in the form of a prayer but wrung out, white knuckled.

"Your mother and I are getting a divorce," he said.

He looked away. He pushed at his fingers. He was standing over the boys.

"We can't seem to work it out. We're getting a divorce."

He stared at them. Pink welled below the white curve of his eyes where the tears pooled and spilled.

"Well?" he said, still looking the boys.

Mom looked to them too, into their faces. She was crying. She pressed her fingers to her lips.

Weston said nothing.

They didn't cry, the boys. They had no idea what he was saying.

"What do you mean?" Shale said finally. It was 1977 in Billings, Montana, he was in fourth grade, and he didn't know a single friend whose parents were divorced. He didn't understand the word.

"I'll be seeing you guys less," his father said. "I'll be moving out."

Shale didn't say anything. Weston had his head down. Mom was quiet. The meeting ended.

This was the arrangement: Dad came home every other Tuesday night for an hour or two. On one such night when he was ten minutes in the door Shale's mom kicked him back out, while she screamed at him and threw curses like bombs. His head and hands hung slack and as he walked her fists pounded dents in his green down jacket. She herded him over the front steps, along the front walk, and down the driveway. With their knees on the couch and their bodies leaned up the back of it, Shale and Weston watched from the front window. Shale's arms were folded tight over his chest. He touched his nose to the glass. He saw his mother's face red and blown out, white teeth shining.

He felt something like a release of bees in his stomach, up under
the ribcage. The door was open, the screen door black and gray.
"Bastard!" she said. "Stay away from my kids." She followed it
with louder, sharper cussing. The words were black, four-lettered
words, ugly from her mouth, hard to listen to.

Weston put his arm around Shale. He grabbed Shale's hand
and took him to the kitchen. Mom returned, gathered Shale and
Weston in her arms in the kitchen, and sobbed. Shale had never
heard his mother cuss, and she'd never been physical. She'd also
never gotten her husband to do what she asked.

Dad continued to see the boys every other Tuesday night.
Mom didn't attack him anymore. Dad took the boys to basketball games again. He was a teacher and the head coach at Plenty
Coups now, thirty-five miles south of Billings on the Crow reservation. He introduced Shale and Weston to his girlfriend, and
smiled. She was a lot younger than he was. Shale asked. She was
twenty-five, or something. She looks white but maybe she's mix,
Shale thought. She worked with his father. The games were at
the Shrine gymnasium, a small hot box in the middle of Billings
with the thick smell of people and popcorn, the blond lacquer of
hardwood. The kids flew like birds, Shale's father's boys—Marty
Roundface and Max Spotted Bear, Tim Falls Down and Dana
Goes Ahead—and they often won.

At home around the oval oak table in the kitchen Shale's
mother sat with dead eyes and her hands folded in front of her.

"Is she prettier than me?" she asked.

Shale and Weston raced to answer first.

"No, Mom."

"Never."

"Not even close."

III. THE FIRST DEFINITION OF UGLY

"No, I don't have to do what you say," Weston said.

They'd all thought these words countless times, but Weston was the first of them, ever, to say them aloud.

It was three years after Dad had returned to the family, left the young woman, remarried Mom. Shale thirteen, Weston fifteen. It might have been a sublimation of sexual greed, or a kind of family death wish in Dad, or perhaps his brand of religion that made him increasingly more rigid, but things got uglier before they got better. He grew unbearable. Now Mom cried in the back bedroom of the mobile home, the kind that arrived in two pieces on the flatbeds of eighteen-wheelers, a step up from the trailer they had when Dad was a teacher in Sitka, Alaska, and the apartment they had when he was in graduate school in Bozeman. The mobile was more modern. The small, square kitchen, one night, became the battleground. Dad had left Plenty Coups and it was Shale's eighth-grade year, at St. Labre, the school that was a mix of Northern Cheyenne from Ashland, Lame Deer, and Busby, and Crow bused in for the week from Lodge Grass and Crow Agency. Weston was a sophomore.

One white boy in the whole high school, that was Weston. Shale was the slender middle schooler they called Casper, or Salt. Dad was the principal and prided himself on being in charge. The students called him Ayatollah, or Khomeini. He liked that.

Shale remembered a night when a black rock, brick-sized, came bashing through the window in his mom and dad's bedroom and woke them all. Dad yelled to get down. Shale heard the wheels of a car kicking up dirt, getting gone, and from the floor in his open doorway he saw his dad through the angled hall in the shadow of the master bedroom standing in his underwear, pointing a rifle out the window.

But on the night of the family battle it was late fall, September, maybe October, and dusk, no threat from the outside, no sign of storm. Out the kitchen window open fields of bunchgrass were white where the light waned, and beyond these was a rift in the land where the rakish tops of cottonwoods followed the downward lie of a swale. The trees formed a long, narrow S, naked of leaves, but thick enough to conceal the Powder River, the muddy ribbon that traveled the earth out there, brown even this late in the year. Dad had never hit Shale or Weston but for the tempered, though painful swing of the belt he spanked them with. He ruled primarily, and thoroughly, by the volume of his voice and the clarity of brutal intention. So neither Shale nor Weston had ever really revolted. Neither had Mom. The sky to the northwest was violet, and southeast, out the living room window, the straight edge of the land framed a black void free of stars.

Shale had entered the kitchen at the halfway point of the house, where the brown carpet of the living room met the worn linoleum of the dining space, the line that unites the two halves of every mobile home. In the kitchen sat the oak table and wood chairs. Weston and Dad and Mom were in the narrow space near the sink. Attached to the sink was a white Formica countertop, gold-yellow grain in it like small truncated veins. Shale noticed a dark power had begun between Weston and Dad. Shale turned and left the kitchen directly, walked to the gray cloth wingback, and sat down and pressed himself into the corner of it and watched. He curled his feet beneath him and positioned his hands in his armpits. The front door was closed, as were all windows. Because of Mom, the house, the arrangement of things, was crisp and clean. The sweet smell of sweat that accompanied the living room due to having three athletes had grown more pungent suddenly. Shale was cold.

Weston ran into the fray, straight and hard, and Shale experienced an ascension of fear like he had never known. "I don't have to do anything you say!" Weston shouted and screamed in his father's face in response to an order he'd given.

"You'll do exactly as I say," his father said quietly. His father's
eyes were rocks beneath the hard bones of his forehead. Weston
and his father approached one another like warships in close waters, large men, both six feet four, their fists slung at their sides,
loose and open. "No," Weston said, and he entered his father's
space with shocking speed, put his hands on his father's chest,
and shoved him back. The rest was something no one imagined,
the power of the boys' father, quick, controlled, enraged but not
crazy. Shale pictured his dad throwing punches in bars, intoxi-
cated but intelligent, windmills with precise arcs that landed on
the soft skulls of men smaller than he.

He grabbed Weston by the shoulders and lifted him from
the ground. Weston looked very small now. He lifted him and
slammed him into the nearest kitchen chair, an oaken midback
with thick out-facing arms, made of sturdy wood that had no
bend. He turned Weston out, jerking the chair and spinning it to
face the kitchen window and the north where the violet sky was
dark. A splintering of stars shone dimly behind the fingerlike
limbs of the cottonwoods.

"Shut up!" he yelled, his face big and hard boned moving at
Weston, bending him back. When it had started Weston's face
looked soft and young, grayish-white and claylike in the kitchen
light, but it soon began to change. His father gripped Weston's
slender white biceps with both hands and held him to the chair.
Weston's arms seemed awkwardly small in the tight curve of his
father's fists. Weston's eyes were wet but unwavering. The blood
filled Weston's head and flushed and darkened his skin. His face
twitched. He screamed in his father's face, "No!"

The slap was hard and a white mark bloomed red, sudden
and wide, from the center of the cheek up over the small bright
mound of the cheekbone and down to the jawline. "Shut up!"
the man yelled. "I'm telling you."

"No," Weston said, his lips trembling, body crimped down in

the chair, eyes small and dark. He looked neither left nor right; he stared directly into his father's face.

Mom was in the kitchen corner beside the window, beyond them, leaning against the taupe-colored drapes with her hands to her chest. "Please, Edwin," she said, and reached out.

He moved his head toward her. "Shut up," he said. He enunciated the words. Spittle shot from his mouth.

She went silent and he turned to Weston again. From the kitchen she moved along the far side of the table to a chair across from Shale. From her vantage she saw the brown sheen of the back of Weston's head, and beyond him the rooster flare of her husband's face and neck. Tears rolled from her eyes. She gripped the cloth arms of her chair, a wingback like Shale's. She worked hard to be quiet. She watched.

Dad beat Weston's face for fifteen minutes straight. For most of it Weston said no and his father said shut up, taking a full swing, always open handed, but hard as a flatboard, dashing Weston's head and hair to the side. He said other things too, like, "You won't treat me with disrespect"; "You'll obey me, whether you like it or not"; and, "You better shut your mouth." Finally, it was just closed-mouthed Weston, tears on the puffed, blotched features of his face while his father kept slapping him. Weston's eyes remained unchanged. In the end it stopped. Then the words, "Go to your room."

Weston rose, turned, and walked past Mom and Shale, not looking at them. The way he held his shoulders and his eyes— this image, an agile body burned down to the white hard bone— would stay with Shale, through many wildernesses, for most of his life. The boys' father followed Weston from the kitchen.

They were in the back room for over an hour. Mom and Shale sat still in their chairs. If Weston and Dad spoke, Shale heard nothing. Shale wondered if Weston was all right, wondered if he didn't need hospital care, wished there could be someone for

him, Mom, even Dad, but Shale felt only a conviction of hopelessness, that there was no one, only Weston on the island of his
bed, stony eyes to the ceiling, and no one for him. When Dad
emerged he went back to the kitchen, made himself a sandwich
and drank it down with a large plastic glass of water. Weston
stayed in his room. The next day they returned to their places:
Dad to his post as principal, Weston and Shale to school, Mom
to the linear enclosure of the mobile home.

In a few short years Weston was gone, hurtled into the maw
of an ancient canyon. He drove a heavy vehicle whose engine
burned wild in the open air as the car leapt the threshold and fell
far into the dark. For the rest of their lives Weston spoke to each
one, uniquely and in fact, tenderly. And for Shale, his father, and
his mother, the voice they heard was immutable and holy.

—for Hugh Dragswolf, good friend, gone now

RODIN'S *THE HAND OF GOD*
— A TRIPTYCH —

Woman Saved, Two Children Lost
AP—Bozeman, Montana. Mary Luzrio, 33, was rescued yesterday by local rancher Sven Hansen when her car flew from an embankment into the Madison River. Ms. Luzrio's two daughters did not survive the accident. "Hadn't seen a soul for miles of road," Hansen said. "Pure luck I was there when it happened." Hansen jumped in the river, kicked in the window on the driver's side and drew Ms. Luzrio from the car. She was unconscious. The river brown with spring runoff, Hansen didn't know there were children inside. The children were 5 and 3.

PANEL I

WHEN SHE TOOK the curve she felt the back end of the Thunderbird slip and from there nothing was logical—the narrowed vision, a sharp yell, her hands and her disequilibrium as the vehicle cleared the embankment and fell twenty feet into the Madison River. Dusk, the night red and gray, black on the edge of the earth. Wheatlands, mountains, sky, and in the backseat, Ella and Shayla like soldiers, like generals in plastic

thrones. They'd been singing to Eva Cassidy, practically shouting the words to "Somewhere Over the Rainbow". . . . then a
calm, abiding horror, an impact that made her go blank, her
head like a hammer on the wheel . . . and the song now muted
under water.

A MAN ENTERS her room in full-length wool coat and leather
gloves. His hair is silver, slicked back, crisp. He is a good lawyer,
with international accounts, but in his heart when he sees her
on the bed fetal as a child, he admits he has never been a good
father. His only child. A girl. He was ashamed then. Now he is
ashamed of himself. He wishes he had something, anything for
this sort of thing, but he has nothing. He witnessed the two
coffins, rectangular, like the old wood cases of fine violins. He
leaves work each day to be with her. Closed caskets. A mistake.
He had been unable to compose himself. If he'd seen their faces
he would've been strong, for her and everyone. He would have
held her hand, and stood tall, looked straight ahead. Instead he
found himself bent over, his hand cupped to her shoulder, his
forehead on her neck, his weakness a thing he did not foresee,
and another shame to him. He had wanted to be stoic, but not
seeing the children shook him, his imaginings were unbearable,
and when he glanced at her, himself close to falling, she'd taken
his head in her hands and he'd wept aloud. She'd held his face
and kissed him on the cheek, kissed *his* tears.

    With two fingers he touches his temple, drapes his coat
over the metal chair at her vanity, sets his gloves on the chair.
Removes his suit coat. Folds and places it over his gloves. She
has hardly spoken.

    Would you like me to stay with you?

    Eyes closed, she nods her head.

    He lies down on the bed and puts his arm around her, awk-
ward in business tie and wingtip shoes, uncomfortable in her

small apartment. He is reminded of how he did not hold her as a child.

WHEN HE FALLS asleep she wonders at his presence here. She leaves him and goes to the kitchen and opens the drawer next to the sink where she keeps the straight-knife for cutting vegetables. Holding it she considers how small the reflection of her face looks, the black slits of her eyes peering from the side of the blade. She owns this knife, it is something she owns, so she takes it, her own heavy profound object, back to her bedroom. She places his suit coat and gloves on the floor, sits down at the vanity, another something, another heaviness, this furniture, tangible, visible, another thing she has not lost. In the mirror she finds her face, without makeup, like an oil painting of earth and darkness, pale hues underlined in black and gray, off-white, dark brown, like soil, like sky when there is no sky, thick clouds of fog so full even breathing feels foreign, her fingers like mallets hard against her face so the bones ache and weariness takes her and she is allowed to fall to where everything one day must fall. I'm crazy, she thinks, and she walks to the bathroom, runs a hot bath and slides beneath the surface, slides farther down and comes to rest, resting, then rising slowly back to the surface, she reaches, takes the knife and cuts both wrists to the bone.

WHEN HE WAKES all he sees is water, and he doesn't hear her. He runs to the bathroom, gasps. Her limp form. Vacant eyes. He trembles, frozen. Please, he whispers. Sees the wounds on her wrists. Fumbling, he removes his own socks and ties them over the openings, over gashes that look otherworldly and warlike, ravaged, like diseased eyes or mouths, and he is talking out loud now. Stay here, honey! Please stay. But she is unconscious as he throws the bedspread over her, and wraps her like an infant and lifts her as he forces his feet into his shoes. He runs to his car, the

interstate, the hospital, to a steel table where medical servants
pump blood to her veins and stitch her skin so that her bones
subdue and she is asleep, finally, in a bed, him seated in the chair
beside her. He holds her hand, his head like an anvil, face down.
His tears have run dry. His body empty. Broken. Still.

His prayers are lost like sheep in the wilderness of his dreams.
Sleep comes, unwanted, all-consuming.

WHEN SHE WAKES she sees him and thinks now everyone
has died, and this again is where they meet, in white rooms
made with pillows and wires, and light so bright there is no
darkness. Her junior year at Bozeman High she tried to over-
dose on Tylenol, a feeble attempt. He was barely audible then.
Gone to Vienna. Prague. It was a month before he saw her
face-to-face. She touches his hair and sees her arms bandaged
and bound, and when she touches his face, she feels almost
tangible, almost real. Weightless though, she thinks, lighter
than air, and she knows now what she wants. Her eyelids descend. She sleeps.

Two nurses, a male, thick-faced and heavy set, a female, tiny
with birdlike bones, stand in the doorway and speak in hushed
tones.

"Shame," the man whispers. He shakes his head. He's seen it
often but still he finds it strange and overdone, the violence, he
thinks, the wilderness of the human mind.

"Understandable," the woman says and sees herself walking
in her own desires, lonely when she leaves the hospital after dark,
life so painfully minute, and death so large, like an ocean, limit-
less and singular, so precise, but without end, unbound by earth
or atmosphere, no more pain, she sees it that way, and the vision
comes, as it often does, of gray birds flying the border between
this world and the next, the tonal whisper of wings, musical and
foreign, welcoming her.

PANEL II

WHEN HE WAKES he sees his daughter's sleeping face, the short breaths she takes. How lovely she is, he admits, and he is shocked at his desperateness, how much he hopes. Seven years ago she married a man he didn't like, an old banker named Bishop who'd made her sign a prenuptial and left her multiple times before she finally decided to get away from him. He'd seen it long before, and told her so, but being himself he'd been cold, not paying a dime for the wedding, barely aware when she spoke in his ear, viciously, in the receiving line, You are a terrible man. Selfish. Uncaring.

He wants and doesn't want to say how right she was, how poor a man he is, has always been, more like Bishop than he wants to admit, like most men, same poverty of mind, same darkness. Hidden, unknowable. I tried, he says aloud as she sleeps. But he knows he didn't.

Her mother always did. But she's dead too, he reasons, fifteen years back, ovarian cancer. A deeply interior disease, probably symbolic of his disloyalty. He'd been incapable of loyalty. Staring at Mary, he sees her chest rise and fall and he is amazed how fiercely loyal she has always been, despite his inadequacies. Even after the wedding, *she* had apologized, not him. And he rebuffed everything, the same way he blocked her mother, compartmentalizing all, refusing to see, as clearly as others did, the shell of his life. How under the skin—he touches his arm—he is ugly. And terrified. Teary again. Her choices a mystery to him. Her earnestness. He never knew her, or even her daughters. He never knew his own wife.

Take *me,* he prays. The words that enter his mind appall even him, so hollow and made of shadow, and he is reminded of how incapable he is. I'm a coward, he thinks, God has never been anything to me. Though, for her part, she seemingly never doubted. But now all had changed.

He knows she wants to die and knows she is truer to her desires than he has ever been to his. True to true desires. She described herself so at one of his firm's corporate functions, and she'd told him he was true too, but only to false desires. They were standing in a hallway and he was trying to leave. Money, cars, women, she'd said. Even work, all self-consumption, all lies. But so what? You're my father, she said. I love you. She was drunk.

But he'd seen it in her, that love, he has always seen it.

FROM THE HOSPITAL, back home, ten months on.

Days in which she exists in seasons of wood or stone, seamless, nearly unconscious, no foresight or even alarm, only numbness and the cold feeling that all is one, all things arranged to capture and keep her, in sleep and wakefulness, dark, day, her thoughts disintegrating and re-collecting, and she is left again only with what has gone before. She is alone in her bedroom. She feels no emotion, no anger, or even apathy at him or anyone, no hatred, no sense of panic or barren expression, no self-annihilation. She stares at the wall beside her head; the wall is grainy, small bumps on the surface like landscapes, like mountains and plateaus, steppes, flatlands, canyons, coulees, each tiny movement irregular and divergent, flawed as the texture of skin.

Love, she recalls, heals all.

Deception, she reasons. Her face is slick. She covers her face with her hands, covers her head. She hasn't seen herself for weeks, won't look, and would like never to look again.

He visits each morning and when she hears his step at the door she tries to gather herself to meet him at the kitchen table. There he serves her tea and she says little, but she sees how he looks at her, peering in as if through a veil. Since the hospital she's drawn her hair down over her eyes, and always she imagines her daughters. She wishes she had died with them. Not instead of them. One or the other. Together. Life or death. Not this. She imagines their lips and small faces, their voices as they pretended and played, their laughter. She would touch them with her fingertips, kiss and caress each face, reassure and speak good words, speak gratitude.

In the hospital she asked, Where's the car?

Sold it, he said. Bought you a truck.

Upon her release he removed the mirrors from her apartment without a word. His responsiveness seemed silly, so unlike him, and today when he parts her hair to find her face, she barely sees the curve of his chin as he peers in while she stares down at the linoleum, gold flecks scattered in strange patterns from her bare feet to the wall. His daily kindness is ridiculous, she thinks. Grace never his strong suit.

Each morning near ten he stops by and if she is not yet up, and she is rarely up, he calls to her from the kitchen. And if she is asleep or half-numb he goes to her room and sits at her bedside and touches her shoulder then places his hand on her head. He draws the hair back from her forehead. Runs his fingers through her hair, his own awkward too delicate motion. It is good to see you, he says.

With her eyes closed she wants to believe him. No ill will. In fact, he had offered to stay with her, an extended stay, but she refused. She's glad she did; her skin thin as cellophane. Whenever she goes about town, the whole world seems to look at her and want to weep, and she feels forced to take from them the invisible bottles that contain their grief, while she must be silent until she returns home and lays flat on her back on the living room floor, the bottles like illumined glass around her body in the dim light, her own tears like dark rivers running out from her forever.

PANEL III

A YEAR. Two.

Weight like a flock of crows clutching ledges in her room, bed-posts, chair backs, black bodies angular at the foot of her bed, some flapping, some still. People see, but can't speak, propped up, anesthetized. She'll do as she pleases. She'll go wherever she damn well pleases. In the bathroom she lies on the floor. Cold tile. Her hand reaches, touches the base of the toilet. Porcelain. Everything is gone.

Morning again. In bed, she sees her father walk through the doorway. Notices him. Here again he has sad eyes. His habit of touching two fingers to his temple. Putting his hands through his hair. He'll be fine. She wonders what will greet her. Nothingness, or tenderness. She isn't afraid. He won't like another funeral but she can't worry about him. Water and form, existence. She is formless, she is form without burden or breath, her bones trans-lucent, dark color at the center, like stones under ice.

WHEN HE GOES, she walks to the kitchen. Clothed in an ankle-length cotton nightgown, off-white, she takes her keys from the coffee table, walks down the stairs and out through the park-ing lot to the numbered stall where she parks her truck. From the space behind the seat she lifts a fresh green garden hose, walks to the back of the truck, threads one end into the tailpipe, the other into the thin opening she makes in the passenger side window. She takes the driver's seat, turns the ignition, reclines, breathes, sleeps.

NORMALLY he drives straight to work. Today, he makes a U-turn on Bridger Road. He'd seen it in her face. Best to check and be sure. Say I love you again.

Far away, he spots her blue Ford. It is broad daylight and the garden hose looks so simple and obvious, he starts to cry. He speeds and halts and whispers to himself as he lifts her body, light, feathery in his arms, light as a sparrow or whip-poor-will, a hummingbird, small corpus made of sunlight or vapor. Mercy, he pleads, and he speeds in his car through traffic lights and signs, her body limp on the black leather of the backseat, her white face whiter than the faces of the silent performers he'd seen in Japan or the bleached buffalo skull he'd found as a boy with his father—like a huge shard of prehistoric bone—white, whiter than the white sun over the Spanish Peaks that shines as it does on him and her, on the Crazies near Big Timber and west to the Sapphires, east to the Beartooths, and north, far north to the Missions, all the way to Glacier.

Places bound by ice and snow. Places he's never gone.

The drive is too long, the car unwieldy. He angles the rearview mirror, stares at her. Who am I, he whispers, to receive you? None of us is worthy. Not one. In the parking lot he jams the car into park, leaves the door open, lifts her, and runs awkwardly to the entrance. He takes large strides into the electric hum of the emergency room. He holds her body like fine cloth. He makes demands and he is taken with her quickly down a hall to where he lays her down and watches as she is wheeled, white-sheeted, through chrome-plated doors, and he seats himself until he's given word, late, that she is critical but stable, and he goes to where she sleeps in her clean, well-lit room that overlooks the city and he doesn't sleep, he prays. He holds her hand, and prays.

—for Lafe Haugen, Russell Tallwhiteman, and Blake Walksnice

WHEN WE RISE

"The light shines in the darkness . . ."
—John 1:5

OUTSIDE, THE SNOW came down slow and soft, the same big flakes they'd seen for the last few hours, everything white and new, the world like a dream. Shale sat with Drake in one of the big red booths at Steer Inn as they waited for food. Shale was forty, Drake thirty-six, both a long way from competitive basketball days, yet in his mind Shale was lining up the seams of the ball to the form of his fingers. He saw the rim, the follow-through, the arm lifted and extended, a pure jump shot with a clean release and good form. He saw the long-range trajectory and the ball on a slow backspin arcing toward the hoop, the net waiting for the swish. A sweet jumper finds the mark, he thought, a feeling of completion and the chance to be face-to-face not with the mundane but with the holy.

THOUGH HE HADN'T PLAYED actively for years he still kept two well-worn basketballs in the backseat of his car, one his own, the other he'd taken from Weston's room nineteen years ago after the death. Staring at Drake eating a hamburger Shale was struck by how similar Drake's features were to Weston's, just older and more full of lines. In fact, the easy eyes and open face began to work on Shale until he was convinced he needed to go out and shoot tonight, even in this snow, a longing that was rare anymore.

Shale retrieved the basketballs and they got in Drake's old Jeep Grand Cherokee and drove until they were down in the side streets south of Wellesley, west of Shadle, among the small square houses. Shale was looking for two cheap portable baskets set near to each other in the street, a sight more common in the older parts of the city than the suburbs. Ten minutes later he found them: two baskets only a couple of houses apart, stark in the night quiet, tall angular bodies with thin fan backboards for heads, and heavy nets like thick white beards full of snow. Drake was a graphic artist, Shale an English teacher; they had full lives and real families and their jobs could be stressful. Shale had felt depressed in recent years, lonelier than he was willing to admit, though he had mentioned it to Drake. They were grown men, they'd been friends for ten years, and tonight they were going out in midwinter for basketball.

Drake drove the big Jeep up close and shone the lights on the two hoops. One shot for each of them, one long jumper sent airborne to hit the net just right and send the snow flying. Outside over the hood Shale said, "This is the ritual." He threw Drake a basketball. "See if you can make it with the pressure on, only one chance to win, everything on the line. If you do, all the snow flies at once. It's beautiful."

"I bet it is," Drake said as he eyed the basket closest to him.

"You only get one, though. One shot to win it all. If you miss, you get nothing."

"Yeah, okay," said Drake. "I get it."

But Shale didn't think Drake got it. He's not serious enough, he thought. He's too happy.

They took their positions, Shale at the far hoop, Drake nearer the Jeep.

"Take a deep one," Shale called. "Gets the best effect."

They were both talented ballplayers at one time, but life was life now, thought Shale. Painful how it seemed there were no real games left, or no games allowed. In tandem from twenty-five feet out, from separate places at separate hoops, they let it ride, two dark orbs that glinted high in the air and came down swift and sure.

THERE IS A HIGHWAY, the interstate east through Idaho, where dawn is a light from the border on, from the passes, Fourth of July, and Lookout, a light that illumines and carries far but remains unseen until he closes his eyes and he crests the apex under the blue "Welcome to Montana" sign, riding the downslant to a wilderness more oceanic than earthlike, a manifold vastness of timber, the trees in wide swells and up again in lifts that ascend in swaths of shadow and the shadow of shadows until the woodland stops and the vault of sky becomes morning. Weston, alone and in their father's car, sped from the edge of that highway in darkness and blew out the metal guardrail and warped the steel so it reached after the car like a strange hand through which the known world passes, the heavy dark Chevelle like a shot star, headlights that put beams in the night until the chassis turned and the car became an untethered creature that fell and broke itself on the valley floor. The moment sticks in Shale's mind, always has, no one having seen anything but the aftermath and silence, and down inside the wreckage a pale arm from the window, almost translucent, like a thread leading back to what was forsaken.

So common for Montana, driving the passes in winter, and so unnecessary, Shale thought. Even if it was a half-baked offer from the Supersonics, in Seattle, saying they'd take a look at

Weston if he'd get himself over there. And did the family think of flying him? No chance. No money, and Shale thought, now we'd give anything.

DRAKE'S SHOT TOOK a flat arc, missed, and rolled to a stop. Shale's ball clanged too and caromed across the street.

"Oh well," Drake said.

"So much for that," said Shale.

They retrieved the basketballs and missed three or four more times, banging out holes in the ring of snow around the rim and dislodging some from the net. Finally they each rattled one in, but the effect was gone. This being Drake's first time, Shale could see it was nothing to him, just something to pass the evening, and Shale wished he could convince Drake how special it is when you hit it on the first try. Either that or be more like Drake himself, less bound by things. Then a person wouldn't have to feel the emptiness.

IN THE EARLY 80s Weston was a six-foot-four leaper, some said the best in the west, often compared to players from teams famous for high flyers such as UNLV and Jarvis Basnight, and earlier, Louisville with Dr. Dunkenstein (Darrel Griffith), and Houston with Clyde the Glide, Michael Young, and the other names notorious to Phi Slamma Jamma. Weston was a swing-man slasher with a forty-five-inch vertical. He went over three men in a game against University of the Pacific, full speed on a dead run from the left wing to the lane as he launched off one foot, cupped the ball high in the tomahawk, spread his legs wide, and brought it down on top of all of them. His head hit the backboard, sent a gasp through the crowd of six thousand, and messed his hair up some. He walked to the line, brushing it off as he matted his hair back down, nonchalant.

"That was the best dunk I've ever seen," Shale told him in the locker room.

Weston had come from the shower, a white towel around his waist. He turned his back to Shale and pointed to a cut beneath the shoulder blade, a clean red line. "Backboard," he said, an indication of how high he'd really gone.

That sort of thing made the young players worship him, but Weston was quiet when it came down to it. Always quiet with regard to himself, thought Shale, though he knew Weston's gift was something most people had never before witnessed and would likely never see again.

Shale and Weston were both stick thin. The family itself was distant, but basketball held the brothers together. As a boy Shale felt they existed in a nearly rootless way, he and Weston like pale windblown trees in a barren land. Their father's land to be precise, the land of a high school basketball coach. He led the family to Alaska and back, then crisscrossed Montana, moving seven times before Shale was fourteen, in pursuit of the basketball dynasty—the team that would reach the top with Shale's dad at the helm and make something happen that would be remembered forever. His father had been trying to accomplish that since before Shale was born and it got flint hard at times, the rigidity of how he handled things.

"LET'S TRY AGAIN," Drake said, and Shale agreed as he stared out the side window.

"Where to?" Drake said.

Shale motioned in a circle. "Should be some close by." They drove for thirty minutes on a slow pace as they checked up and down the cross streets and found nothing, just singular hoops here and there until they rounded the corner of L Street all the way west by Highland Drive. Here they saw two hoops again, though much farther apart, nearly an entire block between them. "Good enough," said Shale, and Drake lined up the car lights.

"I'll take the far one," Shale said, and he walked until he was positioned where he wanted to be, solitary, in the distance. He had felt down while driving, almost like giving up, but now that he was outside he felt all right. So far from the car it was mostly dark. The net was perfect, filled with white, and atop the rim a thick ring of snow was set like a crown in the naked light.

"Ready?" Drake called.

"Ready," Shale answered.

From deep back again they lofted their jumpers, Drake's ball a flash of light caught in the car's headlights, Shale's a shadow in the far darkness.

BY THE TIME Shale reached high school, both he and Weston had the dream, Weston already on his way to the top, Shale two years younger and trying to learn everything he could. They'd received the dream first from their father, then from the rez, the Northern Cheyenne rez in southeast Montana—and they'd both lost it late. Both made it to the D-1 level, both had opportunity to play overseas, but neither made the league. Close—Weston had died on his way to Seattle for his shot at the NBA; and Shale two years later, numb but with an anger that was making him great, had developed a deep jumper, a vertical nearly as high as Weston's, and rez-style moves. He had a slim chance with the Phoenix Suns organization in an L.A. summer league, but nothing came of it.

After Weston died, Shale spent the early years trying to remember the good things. The two state championships in Livingston at Park High, one first as a sophomore with Weston, then two years later as a senior with his own group, a band of runners, Indian-style, that averaged nearly ninety points a game. They took the title in what sportswriters still refer to as the greatest

game in Montana history, a 99–97 double-overtime thriller in
'85 at Montana State, the Brick Breeden Fieldhouse, the Max
Worthington Arena, before a crowd of ten thousand.

Shale would take himself down inside the dream, chest pressed
to the back of the seat, as he stared out the back of the bus. The
postgame show was blaring over the loudspeaker, everyone still
whooping and hollering. "We're comin home!" the radio man
yelled, "We're coming home!" and from the wide back window
Shale saw a line of cars miles long and lit up, snaking from the
flat before Livingston all the way up the pass to Bozeman. Weston
was back there, following him, alive. The dream of a dream, the
Blackfeet and the Crow, and the Northern Cheyenne, the white
boys, the enemies and the friends, the clean line of basketball
walking them out toward skeletal hoops in the dead of winter,
the hollow in their eyes lonely, but lovely in its way.

THEIR SHOOTING ARMS were in the air and they were hopeful, but Drake and Shale failed again and Shale took it hard,
each new miss shaking the standard, the misses reminding him
how difficult it is to recapture what's been lost, perhaps impossible. On Drake's fifth attempt he made the shot, Shale on his
seventh. "I used to be a shooter," Shale said.

"Oh well," Drake said. "We can't stop on that note."

"All right," Shale said, but he didn't feel like going on.

They got in the car and Drake said, "Where to now?" again,
and Shale looked over and said, "To the east side," and even as
they turned east on Wellesley and headed for Hilyard, the poor
side, the black, seemingly desperate side of town, Shale knew
they'd find plenty of good hoops and he felt at home coming
this way. He and Weston played most of their lives with Indians
in Montana, Crows and Cheyennes, Blackfeet, Assiniboine-
Sioux; and most of their college and postcollege years they'd
played with a black-white mix, mostly black with a little white;

he'd been in gyms in L.A. when he was the only white boy there. More often than not in those years, Shale felt black himself, and mourning his brother he suspected some vast core of blackness in Weston when he considered Weston's huge vertical and how he could defend and score. It was a joke both black and white kept alive: anyone that had moves or could jump out of the gym was black, no matter the skin color. Anyone that couldn't was white.

A few blocks beyond Nevada on the east side of town the sky was still filled with snow and as they turned down a side street they found a country all its own, a basketball country with its own citizens—nearly every house had a hoop in the street, a multitude of tall metal structures from here to the vanishing point.

"Wow." Drake's mouth was open. "Shooter's paradise."

"I know," said Shale.

Shale held Weston's basketball in his hands, the smooth leather a feeling for which he never grew weary.

"Strange," Drake said.

"What?"

"Look at that." He motioned to the nearest hoop. Little snow in the net, and little on the rim. And every hoop nearby the same. "People playing, even this late?" Drake ventured.

"Yep." Shale stared down the street. "Turn the car off," he said.

Drake did and Shale rolled down the window. "Hear that," Shale said.

"I do," said Drake. "Basketballs, bouncing."

"People laughing," said Shale.

Drake started the engine and they drove past a small pickup game in the park, even now, past midnight, and saw in the side streets groups of two or three shooting, scoring, defending. "Unreal," Drake said.

"Keep going," said Shale, and they came to a dark street and when they positioned the car lights and turned off the engine all was quiet. Two baskets stood next to each other, side by side, not twenty feet apart. Even now, he could lose focus when thoughts of Weston came up. Bright-lit hoops. Behind and to the side only darkness.

They sat in the heat of the car and stared out. Shale was seventeen years old, alone in his tiny bedroom in the single-wide trailer in Livingston, warm under a weight of quilts as he thought of Weston, and home.

OUT IN THE NIGHT the snow falls and casts small shadows on the wall. In the main part of the trailer the woodstove burns. Shale is a senior at Park High. It is deep winter, a thin smell of smoke in the air, the sharp scent of pine faint through his window from the outside. He isn't sleeping. He smells the oil of his hands in the leather of the basketball near his head. He's too small, they say, Old Man Mitchell at the drugstore, Evans down at the school. Say he'll never make it, but he doesn't care. He's just missing the rez, Northern Cheyenne, and he wishes he could bring it to Park High, or at least Lafe Haugen, or Russell Tallwhiteman, or Richard American Horse, or maybe Blake Walksnice with his little side push shot that hits the net in a fast pop because it flies on a straight line, lacking any arc.

Last time his dad discovered him he shook Shale by the shoulders, yelled at him, and grounded him to his bedroom for a week. He's no match for his dad, but when Shale creeps to the living room, and draws back the curtain of the main window, and sees how pure the night is, how good and right the snow, inside him everything grows calm. On such a night, he has to go. Weston is thirty miles away in Bozeman at MSU, playing for the Bobcats. He wishes Weston was here. The snow is endless, the flakes big and white. A sparkling wedge of frost fills the lower left corner of the windowpane. The rusted out Chevelle is in the drive outside the trailer.

The trailers are dark rectangular boxes in two long rows. Shale drives south on an open roadway soft with fallen snow. Above him in the distance the freeway carries fast-moving cars, frontlit with fans of light, and he wonders where they are going. He passes beneath them toward the city's heart as he carves clean wheel lines all the way to E Street, to the sheriff's station and the schoolyard. He turns into the playground and drives slowly over the virgin snow. He trains the headlights on the rim. He parks the car. With his foot he clicks the high beams and everything is so brilliant he shudders.

At Eastside, both low end and high end have square metal backboards marked by quarter-sized holes to keep the wind from knocking the baskets down. Livingston is the fifth-windiest city in the world. The playground has a slant to it that makes one basket lower than the other. The low end is nine feet ten inches high, and they all come here to throw down in the summer. Too small, they say, but they don't know. Inside outside, between the legs, behind the back, cross it up, skip to my lou, fake and go, doesn't matter, any of these lose the defender. Then Shale rises up and throws down. Shale and the other ballers rigged a breakaway on the rim, and because of the way they hang on it in the summer, their hands get thick and tough. They can all dunk now, so the breakaway is a necessity, a spring-loaded rim made to handle the power of power dunks. It came into being after Darrel Dawkins, nicknamed Chocolate Thunder, broke two of the big glass backboards in the NBA. On the first one Dawkins's force was so immense the glass caved in and fell out the back of the frame; on the second, the glass exploded and everyone ducked their heads and ran to avoid the shards that flew from one end of the court to the other. Within two years every high school in the nation had breakaways, and Shale and his friends convinced their assistant coach to give them one so they could put it up on the low end at Eastside.

The high end is the shooter's end, made for the pure shooter, a silver ring ten feet two inches high with a long white net. Tonight the car lights bring it alive, rim and backboard like an industrial artwork, everything mounted on a steel-gray pole that stems down into the snow and concrete, down deep into the wintry hard soil. The snow has fallen for hours, plush and white, and in the Chevelle's light the snowflakes gather like small bright stars.

Shale leaves the lights on, cuts the engine, and grabs his basketball from the heat in the passenger foot space. He steps out. The air is crisp. The wind carries the cold, dry smell of winter trees, and farther down, more faint, the smell of roots, the smell of earth. Out over the city, white clouds blanket everything. The night is Shale's sanctuary, snow falling softer and deeper as it covers him and captures the whole world.

This is where it begins, the movements and the whisperings that are his dreams. Into the lamplight the shadows strike, separate and sharp, like spirits, like angels. He's practiced here alone so often since Weston left for college he no longer knows the hours he's played. He calls the shadows by name, the great native basketball legends, some his own contemporaries, some who came before. He learns from them and receives the river, their fluidity, their confidence, like the Yellowstone River seven blocks south, dark and wide, stronger than the city it surrounds, perfect in form where it moves and speaks now, bound by snow. If he listens his heroes lift him out away from here, fly him farther than they flew themselves. In Montana, young men are Indian and they are white, loving, hating. At Plenty Coups on the Crow Reservation, at St. Labre on the Northern Cheyenne, Shale was afraid at first. But now he sees. The speaking and the listening, the welcoming: Tim Falls Down, Marty Round Face, and Max and Marc (Luke) Spotted Bear at Plenty Coups; Joe Pretty Paint at Lodge Grass; and at St. Labre, Stanford Rides Horse, Juneau

Plenty Hawk, and Paul and Georgie Wolf Robe. All he loved, all
he watched with wonder—and none got free.

Most played ball for his father, a few for rival teams. Some
Shale watched as a child, and he loved the wild precision of their
moves. Some he grew up playing against. And some he merely
heard of in basketball circles years later, the rumble of their
greatness, the stories of games won or lost on last-second shots.

Falls Down was buried at eighteen in buckskin, beads, and
full headdress, his varsity uniform, turquoise and orange, laid
over his chest: dead at high speed when his truck slid from an
ice-bound bridge into the river.

Paul Wolf Robe was shot in the heart with a large caliber pistol at a party near St. Xavier.

Pretty Paint died before he was twenty-five, another alcohol-
laced car wreck.

Marty Round Face, dead. A suicide, Shale remembers. By knife
or rope or gun, he can't recall.

There are these and many more. "Too many," say the middle-
aged warriors, the old Indians, "too young." They motion with
their hands as if they pull from a bottle. With their lips they gesture. They spit on the ground. Some of those who died held Shale
in their hands when he was a boy, when they were young men. He
remembers their faces, their hair like wind, cheekbones the push
of mountains, and silvery humor ever-present in their eyes.

And of the living and the dead, two above the rest: Elvis Old
Bull and Jonathan Takes Enemy, at Lodge Grass, at Hardin.
They were players in the eighties, and Shale with them. Elvis was
three-time MVP of the state tournament: ambidextrous, master
passer, prolific scorer. And of Takes Enemy it was said he ran
with horses when he ran the hardwood. Hardin High was win-
less the year before he came, but playing point and shooting
guard over the course of four years he created a powerhouse. The
people followed him in big yellow buses, the old men speaking

his name in a whisper, the grandmothers in native dress muttering hexes to his foes.

Shale stares at the rim; the high beams have made everything new.

Atop the rim the snow has settled in a soft white circle.

DRAKE AND SHALE, DOWN in the dark of the city, two hoops lit by the lights of the Grand Cherokee.

"This is it," Drake said.

"Yes," said Shale. The nets had collected snow for hours; over each rim a band of snow had formed, six or eight inches high. The street was luminous, the architecture of each hoop in stark relief, angles of metal covered in white, everything sparkling of winter and light.

It was 1:00 a.m.

"Let's make this the last," Shale said.

"Agreed," said Drake.

They got out, quietly closed their car doors, and moved into position, each of them a step farther back than normal. Twenty-seven feet. Thirty. The NBA line is twenty-three feet nine inches, thought Shale. The message is like an echo in his mind, only one shot at the game winner. In the title game his senior year he'd scored thirty-nine points, fourteen of those in the two overtimes, and they'd won in the closing seconds, the gym noise like an inferno. His brother had met him in the parking lot when the bus got back to Park High, and they went home and stayed up the whole night and laughed together and talked hoops. Shale remembered the team he played pro ball for in Germany two years after Weston died. In an old small gym in Düsseldorf with four seconds on the clock they were down one point when he missed the two free throws they needed to get to the play-offs. Freak accident, Shale thought, like Weston's death. He blamed himself. Of all shots, how do you miss those?

Brakes, engine failure, something. The car was so beat up, they never found the answer.

Drake and Shale were in unison, the rhythm step, the gather, one shot reflecting the other, the arc of each ball smooth in the air like a crescent moon—and each follow-through a small cathedral, the correct push and the floppy wrist, the proper back-spin, the arm held high, the night, the ball, the basket, everything illumined.

THE NET IS LONG and white, even thicker than he'd hoped, leaden with snow. He's back at Eastside, young, vibrant, Weston a short drive away, and Shale has trained for this moment, ten hours a day the summer leading up to his senior season, eight hours the summer before, for the state title, yes, but more for moments like these, to rise with Falls Down and Pretty Paint, with Roundface and Old Bull and Takes Enemy: to shoot the jump shot, and feel the follow-through that lifts and finds the rhythm, the sound, the sweetness of the ball on a solitary arc in darkness as the ball falls and finds its way.

For Shale every shot is a form of gratitude, especially a shot like this. He had so wanted to play with Weston at Montana State and all the hours have paid off, the letter of intent signed a few weeks ago after winning the state title. He and Weston will room together, everything now in preparation for what lies ahead, the huge college arenas, the national exposure as Shale runs the break with Weston on the wing, the confidence Shale will need to do well under pressure. Walking toward the court he holds the ball and says aloud:

FALLS DOWN SHAKES HIS MAN, SCORES GAME WINNER.

He narrates the headlines of his heroes, headlines he's collected from the *Billings Gazette,* the *Missoulian,* the *Livingston Exponent,* and taped to the wall in his bedroom. He kicks an opening at the baseline corner of the court and as he clears the snow, the corner lines reveal themselves, and a step farther in, the place where the three-line intersects the baseline. With his shoes he sweeps a path about two or three feet wide, following the three-point line in a wide span up and around the key, all the way to the other side. He also clears a swath along the baseline and up in order to outline the blocks, the key, the free throw line. From there, to keep from spoiling it he walks back down to the baseline and up around the three-line again to the top of the key. Here he clears a final straightaway, deep into three-point territory.

PRETTY PAINT BOMBS FROM THE LOBBY FOR TWENTY-THREE.

All is complete. The maze he's created lies open, an imprint that reminds him of the Hi-Line, the Blackfeet, and Calf Robe, a form of forms that is a memory trace and the weaving of a line begun by Indian men, by white men, by Shale's father and Pretty Paint's father, by their fathers' fathers, and by all the fathers that have gone before, some of them distant and many gone, all of them beautiful in their way.

One town to the west Weston is alive. And because Shale loves Weston, he plays *for* Weston. The loneliness and the love that unburden loneliness are like a basketball in flight, the yearning and the longed-for affection, the heightened expectation, the resolution that comes of seeing the ball in the net.

The moon is hidden, the sky off-white, a far ceiling of cloud lit by the lights of the city. Snow falls steady and smooth like white flowers. Shale puts the ball down and blows in his hands to warm them. His body is limber, his joints loose from clearing the snow. He has a good sweat going. It's just his hands that need warming, so he eyes the rim while he blows heat into them. The motion comes to him, the readying, the line of the ball, the line of the sky. He removes his coat and throws it out in the snow toward the car. He's in his gray T-shirt, and steam lifts from his forearms. The words he speaks are loud in the silence:

TAKES ENEMY SHOOTS DEEP THREE FOR THE WIN . . . MAKES IT!
One shot, everything on the line. The ball is perfect, round
and smooth. The leather conforms to his hands. He squares his
feet and shoulders to the rim, and the gathering runs its course.
At the height of the release his elbow straightens. He lands, and
his hand as it follows through is loose and free, the ball the radi-
ant circle he's envisioned from the moment he looked out his
trailer window, small sphere in orbit to the sun that is his follow-
through, a new world risen with its own glory here among the
other worlds, the playground, the schoolhouse, the sheriff's station, the firehall.

Breath plumes from his mouth and all is quiet and slow as
the snow falls and the darkness and the shadows bend backward from the white tall backboard. He sees the halo of snow
on the rim, the ball falling from above like a dark stone, piercing the white ring. A great boom sounds and snow flings wide.
And seeing it, Shale exhales and smiles, the snow soft on the
night air, tiny points of light glittering as they descend to the
ground.

He breathes and stares at the open net, at the ball that has
bounced and come to rest in the snow of the key. An arm of steel
extends from the high corner of the school building. A light
burns there.

He reaches the ball, lifts it up, and carries it to the Chevelle.
As he walks he is caught in the beam of the headlights and snow
surrounds him, his body ghostly black and behind him the net
moves in the wind, each square clear and clean. The ring of snow
is like a white wreath above the rim.

He turns the car out from the playground to the street. The
city knows nothing of him, nothing of those who have spoken
his name, the shadows, the young Indian men and their night,
their stars that blaze and die out, and the dawn that comes walking. He and Weston and the nature of their dreams. Inside the

trailer, the floor doesn't creak or strain. He slips unnoticed from the living room to the hall, more quiet than the breathing of his father. In his bed he draws the covers to his chest and leaves his arms free. He casts the basketball up over his head into the darkness, and follows through, releasing everything, catching the sphere again in his hands. He lays the ball near his head. Closing his eyes he sleeps deeply. He is not lonely. He is not afraid.

SIMULTANEOUS FOLLOW-THROUGHS and two basketballs in flight that fall toward the hoop, the rim . . .

"Nope," Drake said, and from the corner of his eye Shale saw Drake's shot glance away while Shale's ball came in awkward and hard and hit the flat space to the right and back of the rim where it smacked off the backboard, angled quickly to the ground, rolled, and stopped finally in the snow along the gutter.

"This is fun!" Drake said. "Thanks for bringing me out here." He ran to get his ball and try again. Shale waited and watched as Drake bricked two more, then he walked and retrieved his own ball. Drake hit the fourth attempt. "Not much snow left," he said. "I bet it's incredible if you hit it on the first one."

"Yeah," said Shale. He was holding his basketball as he looked at the seams.

"You gonna try yours again?" Drake asked.

Shale looked at his shoes, then off up the street. "I'm done," he said.

"Really?" said Drake. "C'mon. Take another shot." He raised his arm in the form of a follow-through, and smiled. He lowered his hand and touched Shale's shoulder.

"I'm good," Shale said. "Thanks, though." Drake eyed the rim, wanting the shot himself. "You ready?" Shale said.

"For what?" Drake said as he moved a little toward Shale's hoop.

"To go home," Shale said.

Drake looked at him, then back at the hoop again. He paused. "I guess so," he said.

Shale saw the look, Drake was disappointed, even sad, and Shale was surprised because Drake rarely looked sad. Face of light, almost never down; a true believer. But things change. You can't get back what you had. No one can. He walked to the Cherokee and got in, and Drake followed.

As they drove the road was free of cars. Shale faced the window. Drake looked straight ahead.

Finally, Drake slowed some and looked over. "I think it's worth another try."

"Late," said Shale. "I better get home."

Drake paused, and looked once at Shale, and back to the road. "Good enough," he said, and he pushed the gas, and the hum of the car carried them as they drove north again through snow that was still falling, deep and quiet over the city. They were only a block or two from Steer Inn and Shale's car when Drake spoke again. "Just one more, Shale, what do you think? For me."

Shale turned to him. The voice had been so like Weston's, tonally. He studied Drake's face. He wanted to see the look again, and there it was, but different this time, purpose in Drake's eyes, and dedication, even devotion, there with the joy. Real joy, as if failure were out of the question. Drake faced forward and peered out at the road, the snow. Things do change, Shale thought, new things come. The sound in the wheel wells was something peaceful that worked on him, something that worked like Drake's voice, to undo tension, to unravel things. "Okay," Shale said. "All right."

"Thanks," said Drake, and he looked over again, and smiled. "Where to?" he said.

Shale wasn't sure, then he remembered. Only one place, and he said to himself, It doesn't matter, does it, the misses, such small things. It's not about me. It shouldn't be. "Up Highway Two," he said. "North."

Twenty minutes on, he directed Drake off the highway, then five miles east on Day–Mt. Spokane Road. At a crossroads they took a sharp left, the road following a barbed wire fence with steel posts, the lines well set, Drake and Shale quiet in the Cherokee as the road ascended past stands of aspen and pine, up a ridge, and finally out on top to a wide parking lot. At the far end of the lot was an old one-room schoolhouse. The place formed a vista over the land, over field upon field that led down and away to Bigelow Gulch, to the south and farther south to the mountains, and far off, faint to the eye, the red flicker of radio towers.

"There," Shale said.

"There it is," said Drake.

To the right of the building, two baskets stood opposite each other, the expanse between them dull white, subdued by snow. Beyond the baskets the land fell down and away. Winter lovely and full over the fields. More and more snow, thought Shale. The hoops were about fifty feet apart, a lot like Eastside to him, but flatter, no slant, and fan backboards, not square. He'd found the place a few years back and hadn't told anyone. At night, when nights were silent, or empty, or on special nights—state title nights, his father's birthday, the day of Weston's death— he'd come here alone.

"It's perfect," Drake said.

"Quaker school," Shale said. "Not a soul here at night."

Drake parked the Jeep so the wide beams captured both hoops. He motioned toward them. In the sky the snow was big and endless. "Snow," Drake whispered. "So much of it."

"Elevation," said Shale. "We'll need more lift."

"Greater arc," said Drake.

They stepped from the car and walked to the center of the

court, each with a ball in his hands. Using their feet they swept a small circle clear. The wind was bending the snow slightly, making it flow in bright sheets to the ground. Drake and Shale stood side by side, in opposite directions. Shale faced the far hoop, Drake the near one. Good distance, Shale thought, good depth.

"Together?" he said.

"Yes," said Drake.

They stepped into the jumper and let it go.

THE FOLLOW-THROUGH is like the neck of a swan. There is grace in the world despite such deeply held suspicions. Two basketballs on a fine arc as they ascend, then fall, entering the light.

"Oooh," Drake says and Shale hears the swish of Drake's ball, followed by his own swish, two loud pops of sound, and they watch as the fine powder hangs in the air below each net, crystalline and slow, almost without motion. There is time to turn and see both hoops, and Shale opens and turns, and Drake turns too. A field of light, Shale thinks. They are standing in the snow like brothers, the big lights of the Jeep making everything immortal. Below each basket a fine-pointed field descends, sparkling and pale, and the evening snow mixes with it and carries it downward to the ground, and gone.

Drake yells and Shale smiles despite himself, and Drake grabs Shale and hugs him, and when they step apart, Drake tilts his head like a wolf and howls, and they laugh and slap each other on the back before they stand together and look out. They stare at Shale's hoop, then Drake's, then back to Shale's again. Clear, clean nets move in the wind. A small tower of snow stands atop each rim, high and white, undisturbed.

Beneath the fear, Shale thinks, people reside in places of sacredness to which others are invited. He has thought this out, sanctuaries attended by the architecture of what people lend to one another and raised by slight motions and larger movements

that build and break away and result in things that surpass what
we imagine. Inside him are the memories of players he knew as
a boy, the stories of basketball legends. The geography of such
stories shaped the way he spoke or grew quiet, and shaped his
understanding of things that began in fine lines and continued
until all the lines were gathered and woven to a greater image.
That image, circular, airborne, became the outline and the body
of his hope: basketball. Long ago, on that state championship
night, every hope had come to pass, Shale watching miles of car
lights, Weston in one of those cars, alive, following Shale home.

Shale and Drake retrieve the basketballs and drive away, quiet,
the drive bound by snow, silent, and bound by fate, back to the
lights of the city, to the river that surrounds the city, and into
the city itself, made of winter and light, Spokane. At Weston's
funeral his mother's body shook from her sobbing and Shale
had wanted to go to her and cry with her, but he had no tears so
he stayed where he was, seated with his face in his hands. When
Drake drops Shale off at his car the night is white, the world
without edge and like a dream. Within the hour, each is asleep
in his own bed, his wife beside him as small children come and
go in the dark, and in the morning when they wake they rise and
ready themselves for work.

—for Melichi Four Bear

MRS. SECREST

THEY MET behind a rodeo grounds when she walked by his car, a rusted-out Firebird, and whistled. She'd seen him wrestle steers. "That's something," she said. "You're quick for being so big." He was from Miles City; she'd heard it over the loudspeaker. The day was hot, the sun like a bright yellow plate in the sky. He had the seat back, both doors wide open, his boots up on the dash. A clean felt Stetson, bone colored, covered his face. He'd done well that day.

"Some men are quick," he said without lifting his hat. His breathing was low like he might sleep.

"Take your hat off," Tori said, and he did, turning it in his hand as he placed it upside down on the passenger seat and looked up through the open door to where she stood in the sun. Refined, he thought, and out of place.

"City?" he said.

"Yes," she said.

She loved his look, a trace of sweat from the eyes back, skin drawn at the temples, face smooth in the hollow of his cheeks, hard on the line of his jaw. Eyes like a child's, blue and pale and serene.

"Country?" Tori asked.

"Not really," he said. "Have a seat."

"No thanks."

"Why not?"

"I don't know your name," she lied. She'd heard it called three or four times that day: S. Secrest.

"You deaf?" he asked.

"Your full name."

"Not a name you'd care for," he said.

"Not for you to decide," she said.

"Give me yours."

"No thanks."

She felt like standing all day, and she would, she knew herself.

He went silent, staring at her. Fine face, if stubborn. His mother's face had been that pretty, though more resigned; she'd died of a brain tumor before he was ten. His father, a rancher and local preacher, was a plain man with a massive build, and humble; he never remarried. Tori leaned on the car and looked out at the broad flat plains, to the line of white at the horizon and the white-blue spread of sky that darkened to azure at the zenith. Endless sky. She checked her watch. She wasn't going to talk. She didn't care if he did. She liked the game. After a while she turned and looked through the glare of the windshield to the faint silhouette of him. He was still looking at her.

"Shannon," he said quietly. His lips moved, a movement of face and voice, and something inside him that was the spirit of a man, and it took her by surprise. She smiled to herself at the joy that accompanied her small triumph. He's definitely country. But studying him laid back in the Pontiac she had a feeling she underestimated him. She was satisfied with this too, some things not easily held down. As it should be.

Tori was from Billings, daughter of a banker and a voice teacher who'd married young, and now in their later years rarely touched and never laughed. Her mother wore diamonds. Her father was notoriously giddy around other women. Specifically, he liked waitresses. *You sure are pretty,* he'd say, or, *You keep a fine figure,* his face the smooth surface of the undertow; Tori knew of the women he'd kept. Yet her mom and dad had come out on the other side of it somehow. Tori was twenty-four, a CPA for the firm that serviced many of her father's clients. She took in a rodeo most weekends, something different, something alive. This one was in Roundup, some miles north of Billings, the small kind, dust in a gray oval over the grounds, trucks and horse trailers at skewed angles, kids running in straw hats, worn boots.

"So Shannon," she said and looked in on him through the angle of the door.

"Yes," he said. "And you?"

"Why?" she said. "What's in a name?"

"Power," he replied.

And without wanting to she said, "Victoria," her full name, the name her grandfather had used. "Call me Tori."

LOVE WAS DELICATE, new and bright winged, fragile, and they observed it as an artist might, in minute detail: veins like ropes on his forearms, thick wrists, big knuckles, a network of scars on the back of his hands; her vivid and searching eyes, the slant of her hipbones, the brazen gait, her body a symmetry he was happy to hold.

They were married by a silver creek a few miles north of Miles City. Small wedding among cottonwoods, it was early September, his father presided. A woman worth marrying, Shannon thought, someone to respect: a woman to reckon with. He had driven her to the creek bed in a horse-drawn carriage, speaking softly to two chocolate-brown quarter horses with jet manes and bodies that glistened. He wore a white Stetson, white tux, white patent leather boots. They were big men, he and his father, his father with kind eyes and well-dressed in a gray western suit and bolo

tie. On her side, her mother and father attended and Tori wore
a dress of white satin inlaid with twenty-one yards of lace. From
beneath the veil she watched Shannon's face, his look manly and
boyish all at once as he lifted her in his arms and took her back
to the carriage. He was crisp and angular, not rounded. His hair
was too short, the white line showing on the back of his neck.
There was hope in him. She whispered in his ear. He laughed as
he carried her.

BUT DESPITE THEIR BEST intentions love grew obscure, the
arc of the loss gradual not sharp, almost unnoticeable until,
nine years in, and with a child, it was unsettling how much had
changed. In the beginning, Tori felt she and Shannon lived only
in daylight, now with wounded eyes they encountered entire
landscapes of darkness, their good intentions as elusive as the
flight of a hummingbird. From her side of the bed she watched
him fold clothes. He stood over her with his shoulders soft like
two loaves of bread and kept her awake when all she wanted was
sleep. She needed sleep.

"Mind if I keep the TV on?" he asked.

Yes, I mind, she thought, I work six days a week, we have a
two-year old, I haven't slept for months. Jessica was in the other
room. "Go ahead," she said, and she turned herself from him
so that she faced the window, and the slender line of her spine,
the curved forks of her ribcage, the back of her legs, her heels
and the pads of her feet, became the sheer embankments of
cliffs that she had made unscalable. She believed on the other
side of her body—a body that seemed to her like a wild, remote
country—he was unknowing.

He looked at the shape of her back, turned to him. Typical,
he thought, pitiful. He felt untoward and awkward. He doubted
her, and himself. He held contempt.

Gathering the clothes in his arms he receded from the bed,

and pulled on the overstuffed drawers and pressed new piles in over the old.

"Shove stuff in like you do everything else," she mumbled.

He didn't hear. He walked to their bed in the dark, his footsteps like the dull thud of a big-boned creature.

He's not an elegant man, she thought. Not smart, but knew she was lying to herself. He'd worked to get where he was, BA in political science on a rodeo scholarship in Bozeman, doctorate in American studies the first five years of the marriage before he was hired to teach at Eastern Montana. Philosopher-poet she called him early on and he had opened doors, even convinced her of her own beauty so that she no longer criticized herself when she stood naked in front of the mirror. Still, he doesn't know me, she countered, and pulled the bedspread tight to her neck.

"You're a sharp woman." He slid in next to her. "Smarter than most, twice as warm." He thought her weak minded. The physicality and the urgency of his yearning were nearly gone, he'd pressed them on her before, but not anymore. Now he'd say things like, Welcome to the icehouse, or, A good woman is hard to find, letting her know she couldn't get to him. Yet despite his fortifications most nights he still longed to touch his fingers to her cheekbone in the silence, and usually even if she was cold he'd go ahead and touch her, feeling for what lay inside, the lovely form of her bones, her distance, her closeness. He'd fall asleep, his hand gripping her hipbone.

Tonight he didn't touch her face and she was glad for it, but when he called her "warm" it made her ill. She knew what was next, his feet entering her space like steel ships, the icy feel of them emanating a tangible sphere as he slid them toward her and tried to touch the backs of her calves with the clammy, cold surface of his toes. She kicked her heel hard into his shinbone. "Get away from me," she whispered.

"What did you say?"

She felt the pause of his breathing.

"Nothing," she said. "Sorry." The belief she held about all men, the disloyalty, she had no evidence of in him. He'd been straight and strong, but it would come, she felt sure. "Didn't want your feet on me," she said.

He drew his head and chest over her body before he lay back again with his head on his pillow, his face toward the ceiling. He put aside his dislike. She's worthy of adoration, he knew that much from his father. "You're my wife . . ." His voice trailed. She turned toward him but he was asleep.

When she lay still the thoughts came. Her pregnancy, an awful unshaping, lingered like a sickness in her mind. She'd been ill from the start. A cyst on one of her ovaries had burst and it was a month before she believed the baby hadn't miscarried, was still alive. Then daily life, despondency a robe she wore, and bitterness, her body blown out, and bed rest, her bones like stones in an excess of earth. But when they placed Jessica, six pounds eleven ounces, screaming, on her chest, and later sleeping in the night like a lost found thing, small and of Tori's own making, the miracle was more devastating than she imagined. Shannon was in the chair beside her, staring. She had reached for his hand and wept.

She believed she had loved Shannon. A part of her still believed.

She peered out the high-arched window of their bedroom at the immense darkness, flared with points of light. She put her hand on her sternum. She was blond in high school but her hair had gone dirty. She foiled it now. Thirty-three years old. The year of death, Shannon's father would say, the year of resurrection. Her belief was not so simple. Pressures existed. People moved apart. Still, it troubled her, the depths she'd given of herself, and how far they'd fallen from each other. He'd been such a light. She remembered what his father had said at the wedding, so graceful and soft spoken: that light does not alter. She didn't want to wrong Shannon but layers of complexity had developed. Things had surfaced she did not imagine for herself, and did not, initially, desire.

She'd been considering it in her mind for nearly two years, the idea that John, the head of her department, wanted to have sex with her. She didn't think of herself as a predator, she knew women who played that role, hard faced, sweet tongued, the enemies of other women; she wasn't one of those. But the comparisons were almost too easy, Shannon's roughened fingernails that she'd loved when he rodeoed but disliked now, John's slender fingers, soft and dexterous, and the fine arc of his cuticles. Shannon's pearl button shirts, John's crisp suit and tie. John's good humor at her expense, his step in the conference room, his manner of holding a pen, a silver pen, the clean surface of his desk, the picture of his wife, his two young boys, the challenge of it, how it took her somewhere.

In the beginning he had played her off, joking with her as far as she dared but never touching her, and in the busy season from January to April 15, he flat ignored her. But busy was behind them now; it was September; and he'd been linked to an auditing project of hers. She didn't want to take things farther, but couldn't stop thinking about it. It was the Brace-Tolbert case, a labyrinth of influx and outflow, a large family-owned operation worth more than five million. She'd asked John to help with the VP expense accounts, five portfolios with entangled budget lines given to her in boxes by the company's office manager, Iris. It was Tori's job to justify expenditures. She needed John's expertise.

"HOW ABOUT YOU and Shannon come over this Thursday," John said. He was keeping things even, family first. "Katherine and I will barbecue some steaks." His suit coat was draped over

his arm, and he was leaning over the drinking fountain as he
held back a tie with a nice sheen to it, broad stripes of blue and
gold, his face turned to the side as he looked at her. He'd been
thinking of her more lately. Today she was stunning. He took
another sip, then stood upright and said, "We'll start at five. The
kids can play. Then we can go over the account analysis and get
a preliminary report done for the Friday meeting."

He has a nice face, she thought, an unworried face. He thinks
I'm pretty. She was wearing the flared sundress Shannon liked, a
sheer lavender flower pattern over a cream silk slip, fitted in the
bust and flowing elsewhere, a playful slit at the knee. She had
taken her time this morning, worn her cream bra and matching
cream panties, the cream stockings she'd bought last weekend at
Herberger's when Shannon had given her an hour's break from
Jessica. Looking at John in the narrow hallway in the gold light
of the afternoon, she felt sleek and high in the rear like the young
fillies prized at rodeos, the way men eyed them from a distance,
the two-year-olds with reddish coats or brown, the high-legged,
heady animals that carried themselves like they could run for
days. She was five foot five; she felt six feet tall.

She took the moment, and pushed it. "Why not, John?" she
said. "You don't live forever." She walked past him on her way
to the drinking fountain, purposely bumping her hip into him.

"Oh." He smiled. "I see how it is."

She laughed, then took a drink as she spoke into the chrome
tray of the machine, "Not worth packing up the files though,
too unruly. How about we do the barbecue, then come back here
and work for an hour or so." She kept her head down and took
another drink, waiting.

"An hour?" he said.

"Maybe two," she said softly. She was awed by the half reasons and intentions that made her dead with Shannon but light
as a butterfly with John.

"Maybe." He held his hand out, a playful gesture, and inviting. He smiled. "I guess that will work."

"Okay." She laughed and put her hand in his. "Your place on Thursday, then back here." She liked touching him. She liked how his hand conformed to her fingers.

They parted, and she worked late. Shannon had to call her twice before she could give him a time she'd be home. He was reminding her of a dessert party they were to attend at the college president's house, up on the edge of the rimrock that lined the northern limit of the city. A beautiful home, she remembered, tall windows facing a field of lights, the city, the dark band of the faraway river, and the southerly plains black in the distance.

"Eight o'clock," she promised about dinner.

"It starts at seven," he said. "We'll come in late enough to be laughed at."

"Seven-thirty," she said. "Push me and I'm not going."

His voice annoyed her. The tone reminded her of his anger some months back when she'd had to leave him with Jessica. She was attending a three-day conference in Boise and when she'd come home after dark at the end of the week he was there in the kitchen, big as a bull while he fed their daughter by hand. He stuffed rice in her mouth as she sat on his knee. It was 9:27 p.m. Jessica was still in a T-shirt and dirty pink pants. There was rice all over the floor, smashed peas, small triangles of carrot. The sink was piled with dishes. Near Shannon's right foot the hardwood was gouged, like he'd used a hacksaw. Her chest tightened and she wanted to hurt him.

"How could this happen?" she yelled at him.

"I have no damn idea," he replied.

"You're an idiot," she said.

"Shut your mouth." He stared at her as she lifted Jessie and took her upstairs. Jessie began to cry. He wanted to strike Tori's face.

"Seven thirty." His voice over the phone was blank and cold.

In the end, Tori was punctual, they left Jessie with a babysitter, and the party was the usual—too long, dry, dim, and full of glib words and fine-scented hand shakes, an evening Tori devoted almost entirely to thoughts of the upcoming Thursday night, of her and John, and how far she might take him.

When the party was over Shannon opened the car door for her, and they drove the edge of the rims and down Twenty-seventh into the city, east for some miles on I-90, until they took the off-ramp and approached the single stoplight that bordered on their development. As they drove he thought of the purpose of work and his life with Tori—he felt like a ghost among his peers now that she was so remote. Without her, he told himself, I'm plain. No verve. No fire. They lived in a tract of recent houses that ascended in price toward their own and a few others, small castles over the gray-white gleam of the Yellowstone, over waters that moved and roiled and carried things north to the Missouri and east and suddenly down through the heart of America to the Gulf of Mexico.

In the distance the stoplight was red. It was 1:00 a.m. Really, he hasn't changed much, she thought. But into her original hope an increasing hostility had come, which she felt she could not get rid of in herself, and even less so in him. It saddened her, how ineffectual people became with one another. She was holding a pen, using the high electric lights of the street to view the logo of her firm on the shaft. Shannon cruised through the red light.

"What in hell are you doing?" she said.

"Running a stoplight," he replied.

"You could have gotten us killed."

"Unlikely, Mrs. Secrest." His face was straight ahead, gray, hard. "No cars for miles."

"Do you mind?"

"Mind what?" He drove, eyes on the road.

"Nothing." She turned her face to the glass. It amazed her, the loathing he could generate in her. Immediately she challenged herself. I shouldn't be so small. She turned to him thinking she might touch his shoulder, perhaps his face. His body, hunched over the wheel, repulsed her. She faced the window again.

THE NEXT DAY AT WORK, on coffee break, she sat next to John in the community room and placed her hand over his. They were at a large oval table with four of their colleagues: three women, one man.

"Nice hands," she said and pushed her palm down and let her fingers touch the sides of his. She loved his hands. The others looked at her, and he at them, and he removed his hand and shifted his upper body a little away. "You're crazy," he said, and he laughed some.

"It's nothing," she said lightly. "Calm down." She folded her hands in the form of a prayer and staged a prude look, and some levity came to the group. Frank, the only other man, put his tongue in his cheek and mocked her. "It's nothing," he said and lifted his arms and tried to kiss Iris, the office manager in her sixties, stocky and blue-haired, in charge of the firm's infinite details. Iris put her fist in Frank's way and said, "Get off me, punk." Then she lunged at him like she might bite him. Everyone laughed.

Beneath the table John touched his knee to Tori's, keeping it there. Okay now, she thought, though she found the movement somewhat humorous, him pressing himself against her under the table while the others mechanically ate their lunches. People are like cows, she thought, and John thought, She's easy, and he felt easy himself, but wary of anyone knowing.

ON THURSDAY WHEN Shannon arrived at John's house with Jessica in his arms, Tori was surprised at how attractive he looked, his outline framed in sun, big hands holding Jessie. It reminded her of how things used to be. John's wife, Katherine, waved Shannon over. Exceptionally slender, Tori thought as she watched Katherine. Religious, John had mentioned, very strong belief. Likely an unconscious mind, Tori thought. They'd never met. Tori didn't know Katherine had a law degree from DePaul, having graduated in the top five percent of her class, and that she was the pride of her father, a hardline Irish Catholic and the most feared lawyer in Helena before he retired. Katherine pegged Tori as highbrow, and unhappy. One to watch out for.

Shannon went to Tori and touched her cheek with the back of his hand. She didn't make eye contact and he noticed how lit up she was, distracted and giddy. He felt a rise of adrenaline subtle and high in his chest. He felt small hearted and base, the malice inside him like the outline of an animal in the dark. Jessie was clinging to him, and Tori came close and said, "Hi, baby. Mommy missed you today." Jessie made a shy, muffled sound and buried her face in Shannon's chest, and Tori felt a slight sense of shame. She kissed the back of Jessie's head.

Tori wore a new black shift, of loosely fitted rayon with a cowl neck, sleeveless but businesslike. Shannon hadn't seen the dress before and almost unconsciously he felt his longing surface. The dress was alluring if overdone here on John's five-acre plot in the flat just west of town. Shannon admired her tonight, desired her, and he could see she knew it. Just feelings, he said to himself, and he thought of earlier days, dust in a haze over the land, the violent pulse of the horse beneath him, how fully a man must commit to break a steer down. He'd hold on to Jessie, he decided, give Tori the freedom to float.

The house was two stories, the main floor on the top level. Tori led Shannon across the living room and out onto the deck and stood with him as he surveyed the land, a large vegetable garden and a row of fruit trees at the far end of the yard, the neighboring houses distant but distinct, and the blond plains reaching west in the long light of day. Everything but the land was solitary and small under a wide, wide sky. She felt small herself until she saw John directly below her on a narrow cement patio. He stoked the barbecue. "Quite a garden he's got," Shannon said quietly as he looked down at John, and then out to the garden. Tori walked toward the stairs that led down from the deck to the patio and felt Shannon stay behind. She pictured the tether between her and her husband as fine as the thread of a spider. She pictured a slight wind following her, bending the thread, breaking it.

As she descended the stairs he said, "You're going back to work later tonight, aren't you?" He wanted to follow her down, catch her and grab her hand and stop her. Talk to her. Say something good or hopeful, something significant.

"There's a rodeo this weekend in Huntley Project," he said.

"Yes," she said, not looking back at him. "Thanks for understanding." She put a lilt to her voice to make him happy. From the angle of the stairs she was out of his sight, and he stayed behind.

Changed from his business suit, John was in Levi's and a white oxford with his back turned to her. Smoke rose from the grill when he opened the lid. He wore penny loafers without socks. Beyond him was the vegetable garden, rows of soil, stalks of corn, sunflowers, the single row of fruit trees. Apple trees, Tori noted.

"Nice." She put her hand on his shoulder.

"Oh," he said. "The garden. That's Katherine's." He didn't look at her. Having her here felt foreign. Why did I invite her? he wondered. He thought of his wife, her good Irish features, her long brown hair, how well she handled the kids. Then he met Tori's eyes, and seeing her this close he wanted to touch her. He put his hands in his pockets.

Tori liked how he smelled, like sage and lime. She left her hand on him and was aware of her lingerie, her black stockings

lined with a band of lace high on each thigh, the black thong
and silk bustier she'd modeled this morning in the mirror. She'd
felt sexy in the early light, the quiet of her own house, as she
pulled the stockings high and aligned the thong and clasped the
bustier, her torso thin and tight, her breasts raised.

John glanced at her hand, and she drew nearer, and looked
past him up to the deck. Shannon was gone, probably off intro-
ducing Jessica to John's children. She leaned toward John. She
could kiss him now.

"John." It was Shannon at the top of the stairs, starting down.
"What are you working on these days?" Tori took her hand away.
John faced Shannon as he descended still carrying Jessie, her
head tucked to his chest.

"Oh," John said. "We're checking write-offs." He turned and
lifted the lid again. He was grilling steaks, cuts as thick as bricks.

"Write-offs?" Shannon said. He stroked Jessie's hair.

"Last year's expense accounts," John said. "For the VPs mostly.
Make sure no one's trying to slip things through."

"They take advantage?"

"Not much," John said.

MARRIAGE WAS SUPPOSED to be a good thing, Tori thought.
But why? She was in John's house seated across from him, and
she liked the view, the dark wooden table, and John's face near
enough to touch. The scene was almost too put together: crystal tumblers and fluted wine glasses, heavy earth-toned plates,
pewter dinnerware. She ran her fingers along the table edge.
Katherine sat next to John, Tori next to Shannon, the four of
them in an intimate square over dinner. Harmless, she thought.

"Listen," John said as he tilted his head. "Worse than animals." His boys were in the kitchen with Jessie and the sitter,
their voices colorful and revved up.

"Wouldn't trade it for the world," said Shannon. His head was down and Katherine was looking at him.

"How do you keep your hands so clean?" Tori said to John as she slipped her fingers under his and examined his hand. "A man's hands say things," she said.

"Really?" Katherine asked. "Like what?"

"How he takes care of himself. How nervous he is, or confident." Tori let her fingers caress him. "John has gentle hands, you can tell he's meticulous."

Likes to test the water, thought Katherine. John coolly drew his hand back.

"He *is* gentle," Katherine said. She put her arm around him and kissed his cheek, and John leaned in and kissed her softly on the lips. Under the table his leg touched Tori's.

Katherine opened her hands on the table. "Let's see Shannon's," she said.

"What do you think you'll find?" Shannon laughed. He put his hand in hers.

"Something good, I'm sure." Katherine turned his hand over, surprised at how thick it was. "You've done some work in your life, haven't you," she said. "And not just in the ivory tower." She emphasized "ivory" and winked as she released him.

Tori patted Shannon's arm. "He'd keep himself locked up there for days if he could. Wouldn't eat or shower." She laughed a little. John smiled.

Shames her husband, thought Katherine. "When you're at work," she asked, "what do you do with your daughter?"

"Day care," said Shannon. "Or sometimes I take care of her."

"I couldn't do it," Katherine said to Tori. "Not seeing my children."

"We give her the love she needs," Tori said. "And more."

"Of course," said Katherine.

John shifted and faced his wife. "It's not like you don't work,"
he said. "You still think like a lawyer."

Katherine smile was ironic. "Life of leisure," she said.

AFTER DINNER THEY cleared the table and walked the angled
hall to the kitchen while the kids watched a Disney video in the
front room. Tori followed John, taking the outline of his body
in her mind and animating it to her will, his hands touching
her as he lifted her, his voice speaking her name in the dark.
Shannon helped Katherine load the dishwasher, while the sitter, slight and blond, perhaps fifteen, washed the serving dishes
and wine glasses. Tori and John carried coffee cups to the dining room.

"They'll be in, in a minute," John said.

"Yes," Tori said as she placed the cups on the table. John's
neck was flushed. She glanced at the children, at her daughter's
fine hair and the backs of the boys' heads. John wiped a spot
from the table with his fist. She went to him, took his face in her
hands, and drew her lips over his mouth.

She held him, prolonging the kiss, making it lush. She felt
him gather, and she meant to keep him there, but he pulled away
and looked at her, his eyes darting between her and the kitchen,
then to the kids.

"What are you doing?" he whispered.

"Take me," she said.

"What?" His eyes were wide open.

"Take me seriously," she said.

He touched her forearm. She felt airy and light-headed.

"Good," he said.

Tori went hard to the kitchen and from behind put her arms
around Shannon's waist. "I have to go back to work," she said.

"Go," he said. "Don't work too hard."

"I won't."

"Can't stay for dessert?" Katherine asked.

"No."

Leaving the kitchen, Tori quickened her step. In the hall she nodded to John, and he said, "I'll meet you."

"Don't take too long." she replied. She blew him a kiss, and felt foolish. He walked quickly to the kitchen, as she went to say good-bye to Jessie.

Tori lifted Jessie and kissed her cheek, but Jessie squirmed, wanting to watch the video, and Tori set her down again next to John's boys. Jessie looked up and said, "Mommy," a sound plaintive and demanding. Tori nodded and Jessie said it again, louder, raising her tiny hand. She wanted Tori to sit down.

Tori didn't want to sit down. She stared at Jessie's hand and marveled at the impatience conveyed in so small a gesture. She touched Jessie's head. She felt overwhelmed by her daughter's neediness. "Mommy," Jessie said again, and Tori retracted her hand, walked to the sliding door, and went outside. She wanted to feel lighthearted. She wanted John in close proximity; she couldn't wait inside and didn't want to leave. She went down the steps onto the grass and made her way to the apple trees because she liked their knotted look, their bent limbs nearly leafless now. She passed one tree, then another, and suddenly felt tired and sat down on a low outstretched limb.

She looked at John's house. The lights had come on, the windows blooming yellow in the half-dark. No one was at the kitchen window. Through the sliding door she made out the head of her daughter facing away from her. Despite everything, she wanted to stay where she was, to lie down beneath the tree and sleep and forget everything—Shannon, her child, the game she had with John. She closed her eyes and put her head in her hands and breathed in and out for what seemed a long time. She lifted her head again and let her eyes adjust as she tried to make out the form of her daughter in the light of the house, but Jessie wasn't there. In the kitchen with Shannon, Tori thought, and she turned her face to the garden.

With nightfall the landscape was harder to make out. She was struck by the conviction that she'd built a life but to what end, and this solitary thought broke her. She rose, walked from the garden out over the lawn, alongside the house to the front driveway, to her car. She got in, found her keys where she'd placed them under the floormat, and turned the ignition. From his bedroom John had seen her leave the garden. She looked brisk and stern. He stood in the bay window. They could see each other, and she shook her head, then backed the car down the drive into the street and drove away.

SHANNON MADE A quick excuse to John and Katherine, loaded Jessie into the car, and pushed the gas until he saw the brake lights of Tori's car a half mile in front at a stoplight. He kept his distance and followed her as she curved along the on-ramp and drove east on I-90. At the Twenty-seventh Street exit he expected her to turn north toward work. She didn't, and this threw him. Still he followed, his emotions at bay some, not so raw as when he thought he might have to do something drastic. He had planned to wait outside her work, let her and John get settled, then walk in and see what he would see. Now he had no plan. He slowed and let her car go out of sight.

Tori's fists were small and white on the wheel. She took the off-ramp toward home.

In the house she mounted the stairs to the top floor, the master bedroom, the master bath, to the small office she'd carved out of the spare room up there. She sat at the desk and turned on her computer. She found the website for the Miles City Star and typed in her own name. The search was empty. She typed her name again, her full name. No results. In the search box on the browser, she typed Victoria Smith and Shannon Secrest, and found, "Secrest Wedding on Sunday Creek." The article gave a few details, hardly anything at all, the day and location, their names.

She sat with her fingers on the keyboard. Then she heard Shannon as he entered the laundry room from the garage. The house was dark; she'd failed to turn on the lights.

"You there?" he called. "You there, Victoria?"

"Yes," she said. "I'm here."

She shut down the computer and went to the open doorway. Shannon ascended the stairs with Jessica asleep in his arms. He entered the master bedroom, drew back the covers and put her in, enfolding her in the down coverlet. In the bathroom, he brushed his teeth, made himself ready, and went to bed, positioning himself beside the child. He didn't know what to say. He thought of calling out to his wife, calling her to bed, but he believed if he said something he might also cry. He covered his eyes with the palms of his hands. The words wouldn't come. He said nothing.

Tori went back to her desk and sat in the dark. He's not what I want, she thought. She was seated with her hands in her lap. No one is, she whispered. When the house was still she rose. She readied herself for bed, staring in the mirror at the white of her face, the arch of bone above her eyes, the iris of the eye bluegreen and streaked with gray, iridescent as the breast of a bird, her eyes so like her daughter's, and faintly like Shannon's. She touched her face and walked to the bed and got in on the side opposite her husband. She lifted Jessie and drew her in, matching Jessie's small frame to the curve of her own body. She put her lips to Jessie's neck and breathed.

"No work tonight?" Shannon's voice was loud in the quiet.

"No," she said. "I didn't have the heart for it after all."

"I don't want to hold you back," he said.

He reached past Jessie and moved his hand toward Tori's

hand and encircled her fingers. Tori lay there, feeling the weight of him, the largeness of his hand, the big bones. The moon's light was silver in the room. She took her hand away and felt him pause. She touched her foot to his. She was tired. She breathed in, exhaled. The line of her body fell, then rose.

He placed his hand on her hip, and she slept.

—for my brother, Kral

IN THE HALF-LIGHT

"Which of you fathers, if your son asks for bread,
will give him a stone?"
—Luke 11:11

SEVEN DAYS after Devin graduated with honors from Montana State University his father stood over him and broke his nose. That was seventeen years ago; Devin hadn't been back to Montana since.

Then his father called from Bozeman.

"Why don't you come up and stay awhile?" he said.

"No desire," said Devin.

It was eight thirty where Devin was, nine thirty in Montana. From the chrome chair beside his bed Devin stared at the city again, out over the bank of lights and the blending they went through as the night took shape. He said what he said, then was quiet.

Devin had left in the off-white Vega on three semibald tires and one whitewall, two retreads in the trunk for spares. His mom's side of the family gave him the car for a dollar and it took him three days and all six tires to make it as far south as he could, south and west to the city where he'd forgotten his father and commenced laddering the backbones of corporations.

"I'd like to pay for you to come up," his father said.

"I'm a banker," Devin replied.

Devin balanced ledgers and paid accounts, justified things from a desk on the eighth floor of the Bank of America building in Santa Monica. Two and a half years ago his wife had left with a friend of his named Beck. She'd taken Devin's daughter with her, cross-country to shut his mouth. He had nothing to say. He never gave what she desired. He drank more, and since they'd gone he hadn't slept much. My father knows nothing of me, he thought.

"I'd like to pay for the plane ticket," his father said. Then the line went quiet again.

He'd been calling every Sunday for some months now, so Devin was used to the pauses, how he took his time saying things, then waited for Devin to respond. And Devin had warmed some to him. But saying he'd pay for the ticket, Devin told himself, it's not how this thing would be done.

HIS FATHER met him at Gallatin Field near Belgrade, the Montana version of an airport: two gates, one baggage claim. When Devin deplaned, his father stood in a small ring of people at the west door up on the second floor, in among the glass and stone architecture. It was after dark. He moved toward Devin.

"Nice to see you," he said, and grabbed at Devin's hand with both of his and shook it firmly. "Glad you're safe."

"Yeah," said Devin.

They descended a cement stairwell, squares of granite embedded in the banisters. A silence set in as they made their way down. Dad will try to find something to say, thought Devin.

"I think they let the bags in over here," his father said, and led Devin to a small metal garage door, the rolltop kind, attached to a steel bin that slanted to the floor. A couple of men in light-blue workshirts hoisted bags.

Devin lifted his two out. His father took the heavier one.

"Thanks," said Devin.

"Truck's out here," his father said, and he walked into the mostly empty parking lot, off toward his beat-up Ford. The pickup was parked far out on the edge of the square, just outside a cone of amber light cast by a high steel lightpost.

"Not too clean," he said as he tipped the passenger seat forward to put the bags in. Behind the seat the space was full of blankets and old coats, overlaid by a .243 and a .22. The cab smelled of deer blood.

Devin remembered the guns. He noted the .243 had a new scope on it and thought the stock on the .22 was even darker than it had been, smoothed out by the placement of shoulder and cheekbone. Devin's father put the bag down, carefully lifted out the .243, and handed it to Devin. "Hold this, please," he said.

"Yeah," said Devin as he took it in his right hand. The cold feel of the wood and the sheen of the gun barrel were foreign to him now, but still strangely familiar. The gun was heavy. He set his bag down and held the stock and the wood beneath the barrel, and he liked how it brought a good feeling of things that had been gone from his mind for years: early mornings, day trips with his father.

His father removed the .22 and positioned Devin's gear flatly in among the mess, then placed the rifles over the bags and pushed the guns down so they wouldn't slide or bump each other. The way he handled the guns reminded Devin of his father's third or fourth call, a few months back. Devin could hear how delicate things were for his father then, how near he was to something he both desired and feared.

"I've been thinking a whole lot," his father had said, "about the man I was to your mother. About the kind of father I've been to you."

"Uh-huh," Devin had said.

"Ugly," his father said. "Gave your mother hate. Hated myself.

Didn't have much guts: No good to you either. I guess I get what I deserve."

"I guess you do," Devin had said.

"I'd like to make it up to you," his father replied.

Devin had gone quiet, his bitterness still charged with his father's image. Add to it the void he felt over his wife, over the dying they'd gone through and the fortress she'd made of herself and the child.

"I was wrong to you," Devin's father had said. "No kind of man."

Devin let the silence be. Then they'd said their good-byes.

But past 2:00 a.m. he was wide awake in his bed. He lay on his back with his arms straight as he stared at a span of wall about three feet in length between the upper steel molding of the window and the black crease of the ceiling. Finally, he slept, and he dreamed.

When he awoke it was still dark. He felt very cold, especially around his wrists, ankles, and neck. He remembered three things: a set of false teeth on a nightstand; the color red; and an image of his child, Bethen, two years old, lying near his dead father. Her cheek was pressed to his father's cheek and her nose was near his mouth. She inhaled a white vapor, seeming to draw it from his father's mouth in a long, slow breath. His father's hand was on her back. Devin couldn't place himself in the room. But she searched him with her eyes. Her cheek still touched his father's face. Her small, tender arms were around his father's neck. She stared quietly at Devin. Watching her, Devin felt she knew his desperate motivations, his frailties. The dream troubled him immensely and he told himself then he would return to Montana.

THEY ENTERED Bozeman from the west. Devin's father lived a few blocks south of I-90 in a set of old two-story buildings that lined the edge of an industrial zone. The apartment was on the ground floor, a narrow box with a bathroom just left of the door, then a hallway that opened to a kitchen and living room/ bedroom area. "This okay?" he asked and he set Devin's bag down where the edge-eaten linoleum ended against the dull green carpet of the living space.

"Okay," Devin said.

At the kitchen table, a metal and fiberboard rectangle barely big enough for two, they sat over the potatoes and fried deer meat his father had kept warm for him.

"I bet it's been awhile," Devin's father said.

"Yeah," said Devin.

"Nice fat doe," his father said. "Standing right next to a four-by-five over near Big Timber at the foot of the Crazies."

His father had taken him there when he was a boy. Devin pictured a big whitetail, the brown-gold rack of horns, four points on one side, five on the other.

"Bright, sunny day," the older man recollected. He looked into Devin's face and placed his hand on Devin's forearm. Devin wanted to draw back when he did this, but he was struck by his own weariness and by a remembrance of all the late-night walking he'd been doing, down hallways and stairwells, or out wandering Pico, or Wilshire, along the unlit places on Third Street, where he shuffled with his head turned down over his coat beneath the crisscrossed maze of fat electric whir. It was a numbing he went through to get some sleep.

"Good to have you here," Devin's father said.

Devin noticed his father's face, the lines and the skin beneath his eyes, the lack of tension in his jaw, the full head of hair, silver and smooth, turned up and back by the way he pushed his hands through it. The bones of his cheeks were hard beneath the loose skin. He was a tall man, awkwardly folded into the short-armed kitchen chair, broad shouldered as he faced Devin, more a man of mountain and stream than

the linear structure of the small apartment space. Devin remembered a weekend his father was hunting bighorns on a
tag he'd drawn in the Bridgers. A whiteout had swept in from
the northern Rockies, down the gap from Glacier through a
north-south corridor that lent force and snap to the cold. In
little more than a pair of garage-sale wool pants and a hunting
jacket, he had spent the night shouldering the slant of a granite outcropping, shielded some from the wind. When he came
in late the next afternoon, Devin and his mom had watched
him unload his vehicle. He described the night as uneventful.
Devin had had to heat the oilpan on his mom's car that morning. She'd had it plugged in too. "What was it like out there?"
Devin asked him.

"Windy," his father answered.

"Where did you sleep?" Devin asked.

"On that rocky bend near Leland's pass," his father had said.

DEVIN'S FATHER moved about the kitchen, attending to him.
Devin noticed his eyes. They had an open quality, no longer the
brooding or the sharp anger that consumed and concealed. Just
a sense of sorrow now, Devin thought, and the tiredness of how
he carries himself. It's hard to find the violence in him anymore
or the fear in me.

"I'M TALKING to Devin," Mom had told Devin's father.

"Get in the car," he'd said to her.

"In a minute," she answered.

"Now!" he said, yelling at her.

Devin had turned to him and said, "Shut up." Small words,
but profane between him and his father, something Devin had
never said. Devin didn't want to really, but once he got started he
kept going and it was hard to hold back.

"You're a fool," Devin said to him.

"Quiet, boy," said his father.

"No," said Devin. "Someone disagrees with you and then you think you're God. Not anymore. Not with me." They stood over the hood from each other on the far edge of the dirt parking lot above Worthington Arena. Some strands of cloud skirted the sky's most distant edge. The mountains seemed small out there. It was just after graduation from Montana State, and Devin knew his father had hated the whole ceremony. His face bore the length of it, the tedium. He never cared, thought Devin, about burdening me and Mom with things like that. His agenda above all, as if it were her fault or mine how inept he was at celebrating someone. There were a few families near, getting in their cars. Devin despised him.

"You've said enough," Devin told him. "You're done."

People stared at them now, Devin's father tall and broad backed in his weathered Stetson, and Devin almost skeletal, still in his gown. Devin had notched himself up to get physical if it came to it. But what could he do really, twenty-two years old and so threadlike next to him.

"Get in the truck," his father said as he stared at Devin's fore-head, eyeing the boy.

Devin gave the people a helpless look and shrugged at his father like he was crazy. But he got in the truck. His father glowered while he drove and Devin stuck his hands under his legs and stared out the window. Touching neither of them, his mother sat between them with her neck tight, her face like something made of glass pointed at the road. They'd done this before.

They were silent the whole way home, and mostly silent as they settled in, but seven days later Devin's father made sure the backtalk would stop. They lived off east of Bozeman then, in a thin-walled trap of a ranch house near the break toward Livingston. This time they stood face-to-face in the kitchen after Devin's father had criticized his mother again.

"Shut up," Devin said, an echo of the parking lot exchange at MSU. "You've got nothing to say to her."

After coming in from driving hay Devin's father had cussed her for failing to get milk.

"Back at it again?" Devin's father asked him, still glaring at Devin's mom. "Keep it up."

Devin thought later he should have heeded this.

Instead he said, "I suppose it's none of my business how you sneak around on her either." At this, his father's face angered so suddenly the roots of his hair stood like white whiskers at the red edge of his hairline.

"For your own good, you better shut your mouth," he said.

"Like hell," Devin said. The boy's voice sounded high and weak. His mother was in the corner of the room in a vinyl-backed chair. She had her arms crossed. Her eyes were teary. "Back in Colstrip, you think no one knew?" Devin said, "We all knew. You shamed her whenever you got the chance. Came home drunk and sexed-out like a male whore. Smelled of it every time you stumbled down the hall. Everyone knew." They'd moved out here when he found work with one of the big ranches, and maybe he'd stopped what he'd been doing in Colstrip. But Devin didn't care. He'd have his say.

Devin's father grabbed him and hauled him to the couch and shoved him down in the corner of it.

"Probably doing more of the same to her here, aren't you?" Devin continued. From her place in the chair his mother's voice made a small, pinched sound, like the sound a cat makes when it gets squeezed.

Devin's father was on top of him then, his hands working to grab Devin's face and shut him up. But he couldn't stop the boy.

"Why else would you treat her like a dog?" Devin said. "You're the dog, not her. Everyone knows it."

"Stop, Devin," his mother said.

Devin's father put the boy's neck in the crook of his arm while he dug the heel of his free hand into the boy's lips and teeth and threatened him. But things kept spilling from Devin, pent-up things urged on by the precision of how he released them. His words were sharp, bred from seven days of silence, sent now in a clean blade of articulation. "You're a reservation dog," Devin said, stealing one of his father's own phrases, a phrase taken from the half-dead, mange-infested hounds that roamed the streets in Lame Deer, over by Colstrip, and humped everything that moved.

With Devin's last string of words his father pummeled a knee into the boy's chest and straddled him. He blocked Devin's flailing arms with one hand and slammed his forearm into the boy's face. They both heard the crunch of Devin's nose as it broke, the sound like a bootstep on fresh snow. It was the kind of broken nose that bled freely and it's likely they both thought Devin's father might stop then, but he pushed Devin's face into the thick twill of the armrest and held him down until Devin lay spent, his breath heaving as the blood made an oblong stain beneath his mouth.

When Devin's father got up and went outside, his mother came and knelt by Devin, her body shuddering over the curve of his ribs.

All this time Devin had convinced himself he needed to say what he'd said to his father. But he didn't know anymore, seeing him as he was now.

When it was all finished, Devin's father had shut him up all right. But Devin just bided the hours to morning and when he walked out the front door he never looked back.

It took Devin's father seventeen years and a few months of calling before he apologized. When he did, Devin was alone in Santa Monica, sitting on the edge of his bed with the phone pressed between his shoulder and his jaw. He had his face in his hands as he stared down through his fingers to the floor, to his feet and the way the veins moved when he lifted his toes. Tiny upraised rivers. Rivulets bending over ligaments, bending around bones. Devin's father had called late, and it was taking him some time to get to what he wanted to say. Devin had the light off. From the window, the city put a faint line on the floor, an oblique angle from behind Devin's heel to the far corner of the room.

"I'd like to ask you to forgive me," his father said.

His voice had a fine quality, thought Devin, wonderful in its way, but Devin couldn't give back to him. Devin held the phone out and squeezed it with both hands until his fingers hurt. His face felt pinched, his eyes like knots in his head. He put the phone to his ear again. His jaw trembled.

Devin said, "I've got a long day tomorrow."

"Yeah," his father replied. "Probably be good to get some sleep."

"Yeah."

"Okay," said Devin's father.

"Good night," Devin said.

"Good night."

Devin listened, but he didn't hear his father hang up. Devin slipped his hand over the receiver.

"I've been learning a lot these days," his father went on, starting them up again.

Devin stood and stared out the window thinking how odd it was to be listening to this. It was what Devin had been unable to do with his wife, he knew it, what she had hoped he'd do just once instead of fueling his words with criticism, instead of shutting her out.

"I've been wondering about how to be different than I've been," said Devin's father, then he waited for Devin's response.

"It's been on about five years now since I started in on those meetings," Devin's father continued.

Quiet on the line.

"Haven't missed yet, and don't plan to. Keeps me sane."

More quietness. Devin's father breathing, Devin breathing.

"Keeps me from craving like I did," he went on. "Holds me back from wanting to get ugly."

"I'm not sure I'd like to hear about it," Devin told him.

When Devin was young his father's father had died with a bottle of Jack Daniels under his pillow. Ended it in Colstrip, isolated from everyone who knew him, angry at them all. His throat had collapsed. A passing tenant found him after he'd been dead three days. He was nothing to anyone.

"I'm busy," Devin said. "I need to put in sixty hours this week, maybe seventy. I gotta go."

"Okay," said Devin's father. "Take care, son."

They hung up the phones.

The exchanges had built to this. Him talking of the man he was trying to become as Devin pretty much closed him down and talked over him or ended the conversation, at times just flat condescending to him. A feeling of loneliness and dark intent always accompanied the calls, but Devin wasn't going to stop, even if he knew his father's voice had changed. The tone had lessened in power, and softened. He'd brought it back to what it was when Devin was a boy, in the times they'd had together. Devin convinced himself not to think about it.

DEVIN'S FATHER relaxed in the kitchen chair. He wore an old western shirt frayed at the cuffs and patterned with fine crisscrossed lines.

"Thank you for coming up, Devin," he said.

Just peace now, thought Devin, there among the creases around his eyes, looking out as he does, looking in. Seeing him that way, Devin thought it odd he wasn't at the wedding. Devin hadn't invited him, didn't even tell him until a couple of years had gone. But seeing him, Devin knew Cherise would've liked him and wanted him there.

A feeling of loss came when Devin remembered himself with her. Back when they met she wore trim business suits. Her eyes were quick and bright. Three years later she stood in a sweatshirt and jeans near the window in the kitchen, her hand white as she gripped the edge of the counter. Her face bore lines he'd grown accustomed to, permanent grooves that bent in and down. She wore a look of oppression, of the deadness that comes from a long-fought resistance. Devin missed the smell of her skin, he missed embracing her. They'd lost each other.

"You know you'll be home whenever it's convenient for you," she had said. "Don't tell me about six or seven. Just say it'll be nine or ten, or one or two, so you'll have some integrity."

"I'll be on time tomorrow," Devin had said, but he was lying. With the distance between them he could hardly stand being home. He had her in a bad light.

"I'm sick with you," she said, and pursed her mouth. She walked passed him, down toward the nursery. Then she paused in the hall, turned, and said, "You don't even know your own daughter."

"What are you saying?" he said, not looking at her. He sat in the easy chair in the family room, only half-facing her as he looked down and away, more interested in turning channels on the television than listening.

"You're afraid of her," Cherise continued. "You hardly come near her. You never say her name. You're always putting something between you and her—work, or the computer or that television." She motioned over Devin's head to where the small voice of the TV accompanied the colored glow of images. Devin turned to her, saw the tears in her eyes. "You don't know your own daughter," she repeated with the same tone. "You don't know yourself. How can you expect to know me?"

She leaned against the wall in the hallway, more plaintive than angry, the angular slant of her body set within her over-sized clothing. Her face was flat. She waited for him but Devin had nothing to say so she released herself and moved toward the nursery. Devin kept watching television.

He wouldn't have blamed her if she had already given her-self to Beck. She had been more right than she knew. Bethen was fresh to the world but holding her was so painful his hands ached, and every time he tried, things would get tangled up and he'd fear what was to come, she'd be fatherless with him right there in her presence. He was scared he'd be all he'd been to her mother, all his father had been to him. So he stayed away. In the year since she was born he held her only when her mother pushed her on him. It didn't surprise him that Cherise took the child and walked away.

DEVIN'S FATHER placed another cut of deer steak on Devin's plate.

"Dan caught a bunch up near Beartrap Canyon," he said. Devin remembered faintly Dan was his father's fishing partner who tied flies for a local sporting goods store, Bob Ward's, the Sportsman, or something.

"How many?" Devin mumbled.

"One hundred," his father said. "In six hours." He said it like it was nothing.

"I stopped at Bob Ward's," he continued. "Had Dan show me what rig he used. Do you want to head up there tomorrow and see if we can catch some rainbows?"

He motioned to the window, his fingers slender, knotted at the knuckles.

"Fine," Devin said.

Devin's father touched Devin's arm often as he spoke, and each time Devin felt far older than him. Far closer to death.

He's well over sixty, thought Devin, with me just a shadow of him when he was forty. Dragged and husked out, thinner than I should be, uglier.

"It'll take two hours," said Devin's father. "We'll have to get up at four to get there about right."

"Fine," said Devin, knowing he'd likely be awake then anyway.

IN THE EARLY morning, Devin's father put his hand on Devin's shoulder. Devin had the feeling his father had been there beside him for a very long time, watching him, probably praying, patient as trees with the sun in their arms. His father had taken the couch, given Devin the bed. With the touch of his hand there on his shoulder Devin felt he could sleep forever. The apartment was dark and still. His father waited for him.

"Are you awake?" his father asked.

"Yes," said Devin.

They met at the kitchen table, where his father had some toast prepared. He sat reading from his Bible. Devin asked him to read something aloud. Looking to the chapter he was on, his father said, "A friend loves at all times." He turned to Devin then, gaze of light-blue and gray, affectionate and sad in the same glance.

When they emerged from the building the morning was full of thick white clouds, low on the earth, shrouding the mountains. They drove west from Bozeman toward Four Corners, then south along the Madison toward Quake Lake and the park. The smell of deer blood lined the cab. The truck moved with a loud, firm drone. Beneath the horizon, the sun opened the blue and gray of the mountains, and the pewter of the Madison. The river moved, with the road a thin dark line alongside the water. At this hour the world was new and the clouds lay full on the land. The sun was hidden beneath it all.

They were mostly silent. Devin's father had made and packed the lunches. The same Mother made for them three decades ago:

roast beef sandwiches on plain brown bread with butter and mustard, deer jerky, some chips, a couple of Cokes. They sat in a cooler between father and son, next to the plastic jugs of water. In the back between the spare tire and the sidewall, two fly rods and a spinning rod lay in the truck bed, their tips clicking to the bumps in the road.

"I've got some gloves for you, it's probably gonna be pretty cold," his father said.

From the truck's cocoon it was hard to imagine the cold out-side, but when it came to weather his father was rarely wrong. Devin's head was back on the seat. His coat rose and fell to the rhythm of his breathing. As a boy he'd be fast asleep by now. On the side window where he stared at the darkness, the dash lights opened his reflection. Here he saw the red rims of his eyes, the gray of his eyelids and the black hollow beneath, then the bones of his forehead squarely angled and appearing fragile, a skein of bluish veinwork near the temples. Wisps of hair receded high up on his head, the skull appearing thin as the shell of a robin's egg. His father was right there next to him, but he thought again how alone he felt.

They crossed the Madison on a simple highway-bridge and Beartrap Canyon opened to the south, saw-toothed, backboned, steep from water to sky. Into the canyon the river moved silver gray, with mist over the surface in the half-light. Devin stared until the road turned and the view was lost.

Dawn was a desire, a hunger in the land and sky. It had not been like this for Devin for some years, so clear, edging as it did toward day. Mostly in the dark of his own apartment he'd hear the noise increasing. He'd lie in his bed peering out, unable to sleep, or sitting at the chrome chair he'd stare from the bed-room window. Out across the city, the metalworks would begin to glow and it seemed forever before he could move. Because of how weary he'd become, his feet were a burden, as was the bulk of his body above them. Often, he discovered his fingertips were numb. When he had stayed at work so much he didn't miss Cherise. Now he found this sad.

The lights were off when he went from room to room. No one would know he was moving again. He drank alcohol and he cried and pitied himself for how it had happened to him just as it did to his mother and father. The loss of who he and Cherise were had overshadowed what they might have made together.

Devin's father pointed out the window, east toward Bozeman.

"Look at that," he whispered.

Above the clouds the Bridgers stood clear, cut in blacks and grays, taking up much of the sky. Behind them was the scarlet horizon. While he drove his father would steal long looks. The sky's blood gathered and went out. The morning turned Devin's face gold.

"Nothing like it, is there?" his father said.

They topped a broad rise. The truck moved from shadow to sun. The land opened wide. To the south, mountains and fields were free of clouds, open now under a sweep of sky. The road banked down and left, and the mountains parted. The river appeared again, emerald, flared by sunshine as it blazed around an arm of land.

At the start of the marriage Devin was able like the rest to glad-face his way, thinking to himself it would be all right. He had overlaid his fear with the brightness of her spirit next to his, the boldness of it.

"Come to bed with me," she'd say, and she'd smooth the line of his jaw with her fingertips. "I like to talk. It's good to go to sleep together."

"I know," Devin would say. But the words he uttered were curt and the clip of them annoyed her and sent her down to bed while he slumped in the easy seat with his chin in his hand.

He'd watch television until the night became a dark strength and he'd have to get up and walk. He'd pace the living room, then walk the hall toward the study, then down toward the nursery, repeating the pattern, making himself busy. When he made ready to join her he'd have to go to the kitchen and drink a glass of milk to settle his stomach. For a few months she would still open her arms to him. No matter how late he came to bed she'd say, "Good. Thank you, Devin," and she'd pull him in.

Devin and his father drove farther south, yet always the land rose, from fields to swales, from foothills to mountains. They were closer to the edge of Yellowstone, on one of the more obscure routes where few towns stood. Traditional Blackfeet country, initially absent of whites due to the rough set of the land and more so the nature that turned man against man, the contemplative warlike way of those pushed to repel others, a desperation inbreathed with ferocity. The river gathered and twined here, where it hugged cutbanks and land bends, parted by islets and sandbars. The water narrowed in the canyons, then broadened again among the mountains, flanked always by aspen and cottonwood, wildflowers, willow, and wild rose.

At the bottleneck of a tight canyon, they plateaued, slowing to park off the shoulder in the brush. The wind bent the timothy grass here. They'd be using wet flies, an egg pattern and a pheasant tail dropper, and tiny split shot like little broken teeth. They walked an old sluiceway, then scaled down an embankment to reach the river.

A roar sounded from the Quake Lake gateway, a large concrete hole grated by thick iron bars. White and dark blue the Madison rushed headlong, shot from the opening like bold clusters of stars. The river pooled from the white water in a wide swirl, narrowed, then widened and smoothed itself downriver.

With the gusts through the canyon Devin's nose and ears started to burn. The cold grew crisp, unbearable for a moment, then it passed.

"Remind me," Devin said to his father as they began.

His father stood at his back, placed his hands on Devin's forearms, and started to speak him through the movement.

"Keep your frame," he said. "Firm upper body, firm in the shoulders. Quick now in the forearms. Fluid, fluid with the wrists. Firm in the hand." His fingers, strong like the roots of trees, held Devin to the motion. "Good, Devin," he said. "Nicely done. You haven't forgot a thing." Down inside his coat Devin resisted, but he was struck forcefully by how deeply he desired just to be held by him. No matter, Devin thought, whatever I need, I won't turn and ask him for it. In Devin's apartment, in the dark there is the hum of the city and all inside him a desolation he did not imagine for himself.

When he first came in on the Pacific Coast Highway out of Oxnard and down the coast, then up the rise to Ocean Boulevard and straight up Wilshire, Devin knew. This was it: all the metal and glass, the absolute clarity, not muddled or chaotic, not flat, slow, or wide, just narrow and angular, all of it, everything a straight line that pointed to the sky. He secured an apartment in a high-rise in Santa Monica, an old superstructure from the seventies, a bulk of metal named the Oceanside, lusterless so he could afford it, tall enough to command a view. He made sure his window faced the city, not the ocean, because of the raw feel of the wires and the light, the grounding it gave him to envision girders reaching down through the asphalt and concrete, steely narrow fingers down into the earth, gripping, digging in with their nails. From there he moved away from the ocean, up the 110 to a studio near the city center, then he and Cherise moved together to Agoura Hills and a modest twenty-five-hundred-square-foot home. But when the marriage was

done, he came back to the Oceanside. Three doors down from
the old place, he thought he might find a remnant here of what
he'd been, the fire and the ascension, the way he looked out on
the city with a child's eyes. He'd be alone at the window, vodka
in his hand. From there the grid of the city began, a stepwise
casement of large and small structures, thin and tall, or shorter
and stouter, the sides of them glinting gold in the morning
light, the whole of it as sharp and promising as the day he had
arrived. The sun gave a white-yellow hue that settled to brown
in a haze at the city line.

Devin's father walked downstream. He found a place that
was quiet and slow. The fly he threw went out far and broke
the surface, then traveled down along the river bottom, bumping with the current. He knew the river's smoothness, behind
boulders, below small bends or sandbars, places of slow-moving
pools where the fish reside.

Devin's arms moved, reaching the line back and forward again
over the jade whirls and darker bends of the river. His father was
far downstream now. They fished separately this way in the early
morning. Devin didn't catch a thing. His body was cold, so were
his hands and face and feet. But he wasn't bothered anymore. His
chest no longer felt small, or pressed. He was breathing some,
and he went on hundreds of times with the same movement,
slowly at each hole. He waited, drawing the line back, drawing it
forth. The tension took its time going from him.

Past midday Devin and his father met up at the truck. They
got in, and his father stoked the heat.

"Hard luck," his father said.

Devin stared out the window, methodically eating the sandwich his father had given him. They'd fished for seven hours,
but they'd both been shut out. When his father was finished he
placed his hand on Devin's arm. If he knew me, Devin thought,
what would he think of me?

"What do you say we head on up to the lake and see if it's any better up there?" said Devin's father.

"Fine," Devin said.

They followed the black line, curving again as they ascended. When they topped another rise, the road wound through a place where the mountains had caved in. To the side of the roadway and up in a broad steep slide, huge boulders crowded each other. The dislocated arms of dead-white trees jutted among the debris. Devin's father slowed the truck.

"Felt the earthquake all the way over in Circle," he said. "About fifty years ago. The mountain fell and covered thirty people; they were camping around here. Workers had a real hard time finding them, buried so deep. Heard about it on the radio. The mountain choked off the Madison and formed the lake." He motioned with his eyes.

Hundreds of trees needled the water, pale, bare, and jagged-limbed, naked where they stood. In the silence between them, Devin imagined himself rowing in a small johnboat while the oars clanked in their metal holdings. He was gliding in the bone-colored forest, in among the trees locked like frightened old people near shore. The mountains themselves could be my skyscrapers, he thought, the black lake the city street, and I am walking among the millions with my flat inward stare, wondering again what is there for me.

"Devin?" his father said.

"Fine," Devin answered dumbly, and looked over. Devin's father was touching his hand, staring at him like he'd been lost.

"Nothing," his father said. "It's all right, son." He went back to driving, watching the country in the way he did, taking it all in.

The lake was more than a mile long, turned up by wind, white-capped, dark gray-blue. They drove the expanse, silent while the

winds gnashed. Swells, strangely reminiscent of oceans, pulled
and turned on the surface.

"Too windy," Devin's father said, slowing.

They turned and drove back down, below where they were.
They were looking for another stretch to fish, but not far on, the
tributaries joined with the river, muddying it, mixing it up. They
turned again and went back where they had started. Again they
reached the river floor. Devin pulled up on a gray fist-shaped
rock and watched his father for a time.

"Tired out?" his father asked.

"I'm all right," Devin said.

The wind was quick and crisp but not as vicious as up on
the lake. The sun shone bright, while at the same time snow fell
in fast diagonal sheets, slanted, embodying the wind. The water
was the color of steel and Devin's father's arms were moving out
and in again. He lengthened the line upstream and it went forth,
unfolding until the split shot, the egg pattern, and the fly quietly
met the water and went down beneath the surface.

A neon green indicator marked the path below which the
weight and fly took the current's draw, a signal point from which
a hungry fish might turn and pull the indicator down. Fluid in
the river's lie, the indicator drifted downstream until it was even
with Devin and his father set out more line to keep from breaking the motion. The bump and pull of the river tipped the pole
but the draw was empty this time, so Devin's father lifted the
line up and out. Back and forth over the water he wove invisible tapestries, loading the line while it lengthened, increasing
its reach to twenty or thirty yards. Above his head his arm was
outstretched, and over the surface the line was seamless, flowing, settling upriver in its quiet way. Here, the movement began
again, the downriver sweep of the current and the line.

There was a strike. Devin's father whipped the rod backward.
The line went taut, the pole bent nearly in a circle.

"Hey, hey! Will you look at that!" he laughed and yelled.

The rod was high, the arc swollen, moonlike. Deftly, he worked the line with his left hand, keeping the tension on, feeling the play of the fish. The fish spasmed, came wildly alive, then soothed itself downstream for a time, then jerked to life again. The fight was a paradox like this, aggressive then smooth, until the fish darted in the green-blue of the water near shore. He unclipped his net and captured it. When he drew it out and freed the hook, he held a rainbow in his hands.

"Nice work," Devin said. Then there was a pause, and Devin said, "Why did you treat her so bad?"

He looked up into his father's eyes.

"Your mom?" his father replied, eyes down, toward the rocks, the river.

"Yeah," Devin said. "Why'd you have to run her off when all she wanted was to be with you?"

"I was a bad man, Devin," he said, and he turned and set the fish in the water and watched it move away. The words were so unassuming they took Devin off guard.

"Why don't you go to her?" Devin said. "Why live out here all alone?"

His father set his fly rod down and sat on his heels a few feet from Devin. "I have gone to her, Devin. Drove to her place in Nevada twice. She thinks we're not ready to be together again. She's probably right."

Devin felt the cold in his hands. He pressed them against each other. There was a quietness between him and his father.

"I wasn't much of a husband to Cherise," Devin said finally, and he looked south along the river, off to where the color of the water became less distinct and the mountains crowded the river from vision.

"Where is she now?" his father asked.

"She's gone, Dad. Lives in Boston. She took Bethen with her."

His father took a smooth stone in his hand. He began rubbing the dirt from it with his fingers. "I'm a fool, Devin," he said.
"We're both fools," Devin said.

WHEN HIS FATHER began again the sun was white and high.
The mountains went up into the blue; the sky was their com-
panion. Bright clouds flung snow that gathered in the tops of
the crags and fell sustained, sweeping to the river, to the shore.
Devin's father was silver and brown, beaten of weather and
stone, hair like mercury, skin like copper. He caught five straight.
"They're on," he said. "Better go give it a try."
Devin did as he suggested and walked upstream to a small
bend in the river where he readied his line. He cast the line into
the air and began again the rhythm. He drew it back to reach the
mountains. He set it forth to touch the river.
In the late afternoon they turned toward home. Driving,
Devin's father had the wheel in one hand, the other he rested
on Devin's shoulder. At day's end the mountains had gone
blue again. He waits for me, Devin thought. From the horizon
the sun gave way and it was long after dark when they arrived.
The apartment was quiet. There was a light on in the kitchen.
When Devin turned to his father to say good night the two
were face-to-face. Devin leaned toward him. His father gathered him in his arms.

—for the two we lost before they were born

THE DARK BETWEEN THEM

EARLY MORNING, April 4, in the small square of their bedroom a thin light opened the dark. When the light became stronger, Zeb emerged and imagined the sunrise on the edge of the world. The sun shone to the city and struck the sidewall of the trailer—a single-wide shortbox, late sixties, early seventies. He felt the light, and the stiffening of her body. She was awake and trying not to wake him, and he thought he would let himself come fully up from sleep to behold her. But he was unable to wake himself, still in the clarity of the dream, the clean disoriented line of reason. The great lighted neural pathways made everything crisp and alive, and he slept the sleep of the dead. Sara lay on her back, staring toward the ceiling, her body straight under the covers, arms to her sides. Watching her, he felt pressure in his chest.

Born in the same year, they were thirty-three.

Beside her in the yellow light, Zeb took her hand and brought her fingers to his lips. Before he'd fallen asleep last night he had done what Sara asked of him, sung the song she wanted, her favorite song, a love song whose words now, in the dream, eluded him. Pregnant, she needed him to help keep her back from using. He admitted they were users. Two miscarriages. A third seemed sure. Open your mind, he told himself. Believe. If not for you, then for her. Holding Sara's hand he felt her bones and the tightness in her body. He was trying to soften her, hoping his head was wrong, but her voice became shrill, alarming him. Before they were married she had cut off the tip of her ring finger at the sawmill in Ashland and her mother said she never uttered a word, just went to the hospital in Lame Deer with a straight face. This is no good, Zeb thought. "Water," she said. "Washcloth."

He slid from the bed, ran down the hall to the kitchen. His body seemed ethereal to him, caught as he was in another world, and as he returned he didn't know what to do. In the bedroom the shades formed dark rectangles, white-blind at the edges, linear and numinous. Zeb held the glass of water in one hand, the wet washcloth in the other. The star quilt her mother made was thrown from the bed, the slip sheet coiled around Sara's lower body and entwined with her legs. The crazed sounds from her mouth intensified, and she made fists on the hem of her nightshirt—sleeveless gown, yellow pastel and calf-length, of the rayon blend she liked. She opened her hands, bent them upward to the hair at her temples, entangled her fingers in her hair, made more fists.

He felt dumb. He stared at the glass in his hand. He leaned down and touched her face with the glass and she took it from him, drinking hastily. He gave her the wet washcloth.

"Let's go," he said.

Sara shook her head, warding him off.

"Please," he said.

She didn't move. Her voice hitched like that of a broken animal and it seemed he saw the noises she made, gray-colored as they issued from her mouth. She won't give herself permission, he told himself. When had he dreamed of her ring finger, elegant and tan and perfect? He freed her legs from the sheets and lifted her in his arms, surprised at his own strength, and as he held her it seemed she was there as a calf or a lamb, she was that small.

ZEB WAS ON the reservation, walking an open field in the morning of a new snowfall. The snow fell slow and big in the gray sky. A white veil covered the ground. He was six months into his life on the rez. The night before, he'd been tired and drunk enough to sleep where he was, so he had lain down on the sidewalk outside the Boys and Girls Club at 2:00 a.m. A few hours later the cold came and he woke and decided he would walk to warm himself. The blood to his legs felt better, the movement, and he blew heat into his hands, forgot about the cold, and kept walking.

He found himself three miles from Lame Deer in an open field that ended on a thin forest of jack pine. Still below the line of the world, the sun had started its burn, red-gold, far off among the trees. Snow filled the sky, and it surprised him, the loud hush of it among the timothy grass and young sage. His shoes were soaking wet.

He thought of himself as a child, and of his father. A slight wind carried the damp, pungent odor of the sagebrush, the smell of grasses, the wet smell of dark soil. In a rage the old man had thrown a cue ball at him, striking him on the skull behind the ear, knocking him out. He was ten years old. Walking, he felt the heat of it even now, a ridge of pain at his neck and up into the bones of his head. When he had come to, he couldn't see, and he felt warm blood on his skin. He was in his father's arms, hanging limp. He didn't know where his mother was.

A meadowlark's song at first light beckoned the sun. The sun crested and flared long gold beams through the trees and out over the field. He decided to enter the forest and walk into the light, in through the dead growth to the end of the treeline. From

there he could look down to where the sun had come from and
then he would head back to town. He had started that way but
when he neared the first line of the forest, something drew his
attention—a throaty sound, far off on his right. In the distance,
in the curve of a draw he saw a rust-colored form. He made it out
to be a cow on its side, bawling and straining its head and neck
upward. He thought of killing the cow, getting some steak for
himself, cooking it and eating it and drinking some milk back
at the house where he was staying. He was on rez land, fenceless,
without bounds. Stranger things had happened, like back when
a big eighteen-wheel pig truck overturned on the highway and
everyone cut school or left their jobs to kill pigs for supper. No
one would care if he claimed some for himself, he thought.

Yes they would.

He was white and he felt it.

He moved toward the sound, the cow's noise loud over the
plushing his tennis shoes made in the snow. It took him some
time to get to the animal, the sage grown tight in the draw, and
the cow being farther off than he imagined. When he reached the
cow he saw she was a heifer, and she had given birth to a dark
brown calf. The mother lay on her side, the glistening calf curled
in a ball between her front and hind legs, up against her stomach. She licked the calf, cleaning the nose and mouth, the sleek
fur of the head. Keeping his distance, he sat cross-legged on the
snowy ground and watched the scene. His head felt watery from
how drunk he was. He liked the feel of the soft earth, bendable
as clay beneath him. He liked how the snow soaked through his
jeans. The mother nuzzled the calf's face. Seeing the simple, ex-
pectant look in her eyes dismantled him and he put his face in
his hands.

HE CARRIED SARA through the bedroom door and bumped
his shoulder on the doorjamb. His actions all felt literal, his

choices predetermined. I could be a good father, he thought. In the hall he hit her knee squarely on the wall. She winced and struck at him with her nails. He jerked back and forced the anger down, fearing something darker in him would awaken, something unalterable. Near the front of the trailer he crossed the main room as he braced Sara to his chest and cradled her so that he wouldn't harm the bulb that was her stomach. He couldn't decipher the dream from reality. He pressed his face to hers and whispered I love you. He pushed the door wide and emerged into the day as from a cave.

On the tan bench seat of the Impala he set her down, then ran to his side of the car and drove. She moaned and curled fetal on the wide vinyl, her head on his thigh, her feet on the passenger door. He drove blind, spinning from the square lot of trailers, down the straightaway on Fifty-first, descending the down ramp until he merged blatantly with the traffic on I-5.

He hardened his face and made his vehicle a fist. The other motorists, equally aggressive, rode their engines, forcing the fast metal of their cars. He heard the high whine of the tires. In the air ahead a thick bloom of exhaust belched from the back of an old truck. The fumes in oily charred clouds came on, rising before they went vaporous and disappeared behind him. He smelled the road smell, his wife's perfume, the sweetness of her sweat. He was free, speeding from space to space, then blocked in again. He jammed the brake, punched the gas. The ocean, the blue lie of the sound and its bays, and out far the Olympics shrouded in white, the grid of concrete and wires—Seattle—to him everything was nothing.

On the seat beside him, he saw things he wanted to avoid seeing. Sara's head was pressed to the right front pocket of his jeans. Her nightgown, tucked at her feet earlier, was up near midthigh now. Her hands touched the gown at her crotch and he found in that bunching of hands and gathered cloth precisely what he hoped he wouldn't. No blood showed, yet he imagined her body a river. He watched her fine-boned fingers, slender, translucent, nearly hueless and pale brown. He envisioned again a real ring on her finger, not the thin one he had given her, the one bought in Billings, used, simple as a band of copper. He saw her finger healed, not stunted from the saw blade, no absent last knuckle making her hand awkward, and deformed. In his mind he saw a very fine ring, graced by diamonds. Only what's real, that's what we need. That's all. But driving, he couldn't remember a single thing he and she had ever talked about, or why they might have pressed their faces to one another as they had, why their hands would be locked together in his dreams. In dreams of his own fury, his own discord. In every dream.

He remembered at the start he had exerted so much energy fighting the idea that he needed her, finally killing it and succeeding in not needing her, then staring into her ashen face with his own expressionless eyes so that she'd know he had overcome her. He'd felt ill about himself then, and now he felt out of sorts again. His mind kept warping things and the distortion felt familiar like kin, or the way mescaline bent his thoughts and sent him undulating. A run of meth could unravel him. He hadn't slept for days.

She sat up and stared out the windshield, out over the hood to the roadway, to the push of cars. If there is blood her hands cover it, he thought, they cover where it must be spotting her gown. Even without evidence, he convinced himself there was blood, down beneath where her fingers had dug in, and he felt his thoughts constrict and he couldn't shake them. He'd been clean for nearly six months, hadn't he? Now he couldn't remember if he was still clean or blown to oblivion. Sara was silent. He kept looking at her to be sure and each time though he knew his head was bent, his bulky zigzagged mind ruined things and his thoughts flared. She sat there so quiet. He felt lost.

★   ★   ★

THEY MET in the alley behind Lucky Lil's, the modernized gas station/casino in Lame Deer. January, southeast Montana, Northern Cheyenne reservation: Zebulon Sindelar and Sara Runs Too Far. His family had called him Zeb, but she called him "Z" and it was the first time he liked his name. He wished everyone would call him Z, the sound as smooth as he wanted to be.

"Ha ho," she'd said when he sat down next to her. "Cold, enit." He had nodded.

"Will you get me some more?" She tipped an empty Styrofoam cup his way.

He walked around the building into Lucky Lil's to get two coffees. From the start he loved how she said *enit*, an affectionate word, a connecting word that everyone on the rez seemed to use. The two of them sat with their backs to the wall of the gas station, knees in their arms. They held the Styrofoam cups in their hands and steam lifted from the small round openings, up into their faces. Keep warm, he thought, let the alcohol burn down. She was Northern Cheyenne and, he decided, not as ugly as him. Her looks weren't much. Her frame could be attractive. She was lithe, and powerful, a descendant of Chief Morning Star, she said.

They talked a lot and did little, and in late September, they married on a cutbank above the Powder River, a drunk priest officiating. Sara's mother, her brother, and her uncle Benjamin were present. Her dad was knifed in the throat at a house party when she was three. On the bank, Zeb cussed under his breath at Sara's uncle for trying to take over the wedding. The uncle had done some smudging with sweetgrass and used a gold eagle fan to waft smoke in their faces. Sara stared at Zeb, but kept silent. Zeb's own family knew nothing.

"AT COLSTRIP, the health teacher said fifty percent of girls on the rez are sexually abused." Zeb had grown up in Colstrip, white town, thirty-five miles away. They sat on the sidewalk in front of

Lucky Lil's, feet in the street. They'd been married six months. Beaters drove by trailing plumes of exhaust, broke-down boats from the seventies or early eighties. They'd seen Matthew Bird's old Lincoln Continental, Blake Big Head in his Monte Carlo, and twice Jonas Woodenthigh's white Cadillac Eldorado, rusted at the sideboards and wheel wells, cruising. Jonas rode low in the front seat with only his forehead and the black shock of his hair visible.

"White numbers, Custer," she said. Then she thought about it, looking off. "Probably higher, really." She looked at him. "Sad, enit."

"Crazy," he said.

She looked at the houses across the street and he followed her eyes and saw the dirt yards, the clear glass of the windows. The houses stood curtainless but for a bedsheet in the living room window of the house one down from where they sat. The sheet hung off kilter, likely put up with tape or nails. Set randomly on the slant of hills up and back from the road, the houses looked like square Easter eggs. In the late morning the buildings seemed sleepy. Beyond them, outhouses littered the hillsides. The out-houses had no doors and from where Zeb sat the openings were dark rectangular holes. Passageways to somewhere else.

"Four suicides in one month last year," she said. "Two of them good friends of mine."

"Girls?" he asked.

"Men," she said. "Bobby Scalpcane. Buster Two Moons. C. L. Not Afraid. Lester Beartusk." Her face was matter of fact. "They used guns."

LIKE HIM, SHE FELT the need to get out. Lame Deer, no good jobs, the first miscarriage. They decided on Seattle and bought a '79 Impala with her rez money. Before leaving, though, she said her mind. "Z, you need to be at peace with Benjamin." They were in her mom's house, in bed watching a video animated with talking animals, a bright-lit land, a symphony of sounds and grave words. He told her he didn't know how. Two nights later, past midnight, Zeb observed Benjamin leaning over a sleeping child. There were still fifteen or twenty people downstairs, all in the living room around three separate card tables, losing money at poker or blackjack, some playing cribbage. A gambling cult flick showed on the big TV, the giant box Sara's mother had won at bingo. The lead actor, about man-sized on the huge screen, had set up his friend on a card scam by cheating him behind his back with a group of cops so they both ended up getting their faces beaten in. From the portable stereo in the kitchen, guitars burned clean and wild. Sara's mom stood over a vat of oil, making fry bread tacos.

With the plumbing out Zeb had gone upstairs to relieve himself out the side window of the bathroom. When he emerged he saw Benjamin down the hall to his right, kneeling over one of his sons. The boy was his second born, a five-year-old asleep in the hall and Zeb hadn't noticed him before. The boy lay on his stomach, one arm tucked under, the other extended, face to the side. Benjamin lay down next to the child. He smoothed the boy's hair and stared at his face. He kissed the boy's cheek. When Benjamin stood up to go back downstairs he noticed Zeb and smiled.

"Ha ho, Dirty White Boy," he said. "Any more money for me to take?" He'd already taken Zeb for more than thirty.

"No," said Zeb.

"Too bad," said Benjamin, and he laughed and put his hand on Zeb's shoulder. "White money is always the best, enit. How 'bout we get some fry bread?" Benjamin motioned with his lips down toward the kitchen. The smell of the hot bread made Zeb's mouth water.

"I'll follow you," Zeb said.

"You done that all night, enit," said Benjamin, chuckling as he walked downstairs.

Zeb nodded and laughed. He was good and drunk and it felt good to laugh, to see Benjamin with his son and be given a second chance. He reached and touched Benjamin's shoulder, and they paused on the stairs.

"I'm sorry for how I was at the wedding," Zeb said.

"It's nothing, Z," said Benjamin, looking him in the face. He play-punched Zeb on the chest. Then he laughed again, shook his head, and said "Dirty White Boy, enit."

TOPPING EIGHTY ON I-5 Zeb cut a line between two semis to the outside lane. He looked at Sara, still upright, head back, eyes closed. He watched the road. He wasn't sure she was real. Reaching for her arm he touched a sheen of sweat that made him shudder. I don't know her middle name, or why she parts her hair down the middle, why she slips her braids in front as she does, tied at the end in two-colored cloth—turquoise and black yesterday, orange and red the day before. Nothing today. Why that face, and why above her forehead the high abandon of her hair? Luminous like a woman made of filament, or fine glass. Backlit from the light of day, her body a fluted vase, her hair like fire, jet-black on her head, the shape of it plumed, not flat with the usual ravenlike texture, not parted, not braided. She'd pulled at it, making the root line at the temples pink and raw. The bones shone in her face: her jawline and cheekbones, the orbital bones around her eyes.

He liked her face, and it came to him now in the dream of Seattle, he knew her less, or not as purely as it seemed he had, but he found her more beautiful. He blamed it on the mescaline. She needs me, he told himself. The second miscarriage came a year ago. She's too thin, he thought, her head tipped back on the seat, arms slack, her skin grayish and pale. He imagined her eyes behind the closed eyelids, the black minute disks of her irises, the darker black of the pupil at the center. He was struck by a sense that a song, or a prayer, or something sacred should be done, but he had nothing. And she had nothing. Or at least he'd never heard of what she had, or never asked. The sweat on her had started to dull and with the noise of the engine he couldn't hear her next to him. She was no longer crying. He reached and touched her arm again. The skin was cool. He took his hand away. She looked straight ahead.

"She's dead," she said.

Her voice, disembodied, too loud between him and the glass of the windshield, shocked him. It's the way I've angled myself, he thought, and he moved some and leaned forward more, shifting his weight so that he glared over the wheel, out at the dividing lines. It scared him, the power she held. He lost something of himself. He saw his mother's face. He pictured Sara next to him on the bank of the Powder River the day they were married. They wore the ribbon shirts her mother made, purple shirts with long pink and gold ribbons sewn to the shoulders and chest. In the wind the ribbons trailed behind them.

"The colors of earth and sunset," Sara had said.

"Yes," he'd answered.

"The baby's dead," she said now.

He said nothing. He stared at the road.

The hunger came, feral, like a disease.

With his left hand he drove. With his right he rifled the glove compartment, the crease of dash and windshield, under the seat. He wanted to leave and come back from somewhere else. He'd emerge from a place of dirt streets, from the hot space behind the middle-class houses back in Colstrip on post-Independence Day, where the food from the alley barrels could be had for the taking. From there he would succeed in rising back to where he needed to be, back to the driver's seat for the April 4 drive on I-5 where the words remained like two loud claps, the twice-formed flowering of blue-yellow flames from the barrel of a gun alive in the dark.

It was what she said. He disliked words. He hated them. He wished he could be deaf. Everything is confusion, he thought, everything a dream. He felt the reach, the pulling upward. He considered his own death.

"She's dead," she said again.

"How do you know?" he said.

"She doesn't move," she whispered.

He stared at her. Her body had no luster. The muscles looked undefined: oblong shapes rounded downward at the calves; the thin oval of her tricep on the back of her arm, above her elbow, below the line of her armpit. Vague decisions are the slaying of things, he thought, the cutting off of her or me, the end of something, the beginning of what will not be reversed. The car felt brittle, like he might snap the wheel in his fingers or slam a hole in the floor with his foot. He thought of weeping, and wanted big tears on his face like mercury, thick and slow in the pocks and dents below his cheekbones, cresting the jawbone, running down his neck.

He wished she would say something.

She opened her eyes and looked over. He looked away.

He sped down the off-ramp, the route on Third Street among the square tall high-rises with clouds moving among them. Up ahead he saw the circle entrance of Good Samaritan, the rectangular jut of hospital against sky. Through the electric doors he carried her. She seemed smaller to him now, and boneless.

His grandmother's porcelain-faced doll lay on the bed at the ranch house outside Colstrip, its curled blond locks and blue eyes under the white bonnet. White blouse and fine-flowered dress, white stockings and tiny black shoes. He was five years old. It fascinated him, the play of the arms, the graceful feel of the body and the legs, the face so exquisite and hard as stone. He remembered he had never asked Sara what she played with as a child, or with whom, or what fears she might have had.

The doctors knew. They were as certain as she. He'd scream at them, he decided, throw curse words until his head blew. Say, "How? How do you know?!" He'd say nothing. Stand as a stuffed man with no mouth or ears, his arms and body so elongated that the shoulders narrowed straight to the neck. He'd pack cotton bunting into the back of his own head to fill the space inside his face. No mouth or ears, but eyes. Black buttons from his father's first suit. In the silence he thought of men who abuse women, men with sisters, wives, children. He thought of himself as one of these men, empty and consumed by greed, given over.

HE DIDN'T KNOW anymore what was real; the car idling a few feet from the front porch at Sara's mom's house in Lame Deer; he and Sara leaving for Seattle? It was late September, the sun past the zenith. He sat in the driver's seat and waited. The house, a two-story tower, set a slight shadow off east of itself. He heard Sara crying, and felt nothing. He was always shut down unless drunk or high, and then he broke wide open. He hated this about himself. She sat upright on her knees in the entryway. She clutched two of her nieces to her chest, a seven-year-old and a four-year-old. They touched her eyes as she cried. The younger one looked confused. The older appeared curious and she kissed Sara's cheek. "Salty," she said, and smiled.

Zeb watched the scene, glad to be free of family, not hers so much, but his—his father especially, the way the old man burned every bridge.

Sara took her time, and Zeb thought it brave, how hard people have to work to make something new. He'd left Colstrip at fifteen and hitchhiked to Lame Deer, thinking he would be white and weird, but largely unthreatened, as he had been in the summers when he worked the fireworks booths at Jimtown near the rez line. And people had taken him in, parents or uncles or aunts of friends he'd made at parties or at the odd jobs he held—fireworks in early summer, driving swather or shucking bales through August, pumping gas in the dead months of winter. Most of his host families didn't seem to care if he came or went, white boy walking from the bright HUD houses. They hardly noticed, and Zeb had preferred it that way. Dirty White Boy, the older crowd called him, after the Foreigner song from *Head Games*. He liked that. But being white, and not pretty, he'd had to guard his own back when he was out late and the drink and drug reached full tilt.

Sara kissed her nieces' hands, sat down cross-legged, and took both children on her lap. She began singing them a song.

Please, he thought. He sighed and settled back in the seat.

He looked up. The sun traveled soft and white and high. Early on, he had thought of her only rarely. He'd heard she and her mom were back from living ten years on the Sioux rez in Wolf Point. He'd seen Sara in town, but she always ran with Clifford Black Eagle, a Crow boy she'd met in school at St. Labre. Then Clifford moved to the Yakama rez in Washington. Zeb's father had died the same year and Zeb mentioned it to her when they had coffee that first time. Montana Highway Patrol found the old man dead in a ditch on a dirt road five miles south of Colstrip. No one but Zeb's mom attended the funeral.

"Did you like your dad?" Sara had asked him.

"No," he'd said.

"Did you care if he died?"

"Fine with me," he said.

"Really?" she asked.

ON THE DRIVE WEST, she spent the first five or six hours crying or sleeping. She'd turned herself from him and he couldn't see her eyes, but he envisioned the dark sockets, the eyes burned

out. Her body leaned into the armrest. She rested her cheek on
the bumper of the side window and stared away north. So petite,
he thought, so full of sorrows. She sat this way for a great while,
looking over the long white bench of the plains, over the rise of
the land, the mountains.

Nine hours in, he said, "We can go back." They had crossed
the Great Divide near Butte and were past Missoula, on the upswing of Lolo Pass. Seattle waited, still only a dream. In the dark
before Idaho, the high beams of the Impala shone like pale arms.
To their left, the span of forest was endless. A low unseen moon
opened the sky behind the mountains. He pictured tamaracks
among the greater forest; he'd seen them in the light before
dark, firing the land with their bright burnt orange. They passed
high dark pines at the roadside, lodgepoles, eerily individualized,
bands of onlookers peering over, looking in.

"I'm just sad," she'd said.

But the first day in Seattle she had looked in the paper, made
a call, and landed a cheap rental off I-5, close to downtown. He'd
brought her here for opportunity, though what they found was
hardly better: him at the Vietnamese market up Fifty-first, her
taking the bus to Pike's each morning to sell bracelets she wove
from colored thread. They threaded things with television, alcohol, and the drugs they could find, mostly mescaline, speed, and
methadone. Easy to be invisible, he thought, so many people
in the streets, a thousand vagabonds for every ten miles of city,
most of them Anglo and hollow-eyed. People stare, he told himself, but I'm less conspicuous, though he knew he looked polar
white and pocked up, his face gray-dented as the moon.

Two years in he found himself in the hull of the trailer at
night, in an easy chair a short reach from the television. He liked
the chamber dark, the length of his body encased in the bloom
of light from the TV. "Too loud," she'd say from the back, and
he'd click the volume down with the remote.

He liked her voice, an edgy voice from down the hall, weary

from the day and drifting off. It reminded him of the acidic, hateful way she came at him back in Lame Deer when he walked on her. It didn't matter if they were in private or public, she'd tell him to shut up and curse him until he backed off. She'd call him Custer, or Evans, or some other white idiot from the past. Scratch his face, grab a fistful of hair. She'd jump on his back if she felt she had to, but mostly only when she was drunk. He would pull her off, and she'd calm if he said he was sorry. It was a mess if he didn't. Once he had thought he might have to kill her. It hadn't happened in a long time and he missed her quick anger, her fire.

He'd turn the volume down, and when he heard the sighs of her breathing again he'd push it back up. Broke, but they had cable. Had to have cable, he thought, to stay human. He'd get suspended in the globe of light the TV emitted and the thoughts would get him, images of Lame Deer and her family. He hated it but he'd go back to it, like a woman wearing long sleeves over the wounding she's done. Draw the sleeve back and make it bleed; hide when others draw near. The memories pierced him like that, opening his skin, making him feel something akin to love, but more the shadow of love; a promise consumed by emptiness; a self to which he felt he had always been bound, lonely, embittered, at enmity with all; the question for which he'd found no answer; the old sorrow come again to make a home in him.

The mixture of how she loved children, the lack he felt inside, and the visions he carried of her and him, of what they might be as parents, kept him going despite the walls he'd found between them. Three years worth. Two gifts gone. One lost here, one back on the reservation. Two deaths, though he reasoned they were only miscarriages, and early ones. And now she was pregnant again, and nearly full term, five months further than they'd gone before, and carrying the child they called Rachel, the child of their patience, their peace.

★ ★ ★

HE SAW the doctor's head, the mouth moving: *I'm sorry, sir, the baby's dead. We'll have to deliver it. Wait here. We'll tell you when the procedure's over.*

Zeb viewed the room through the heightened vision that came with doing speed. But he wasn't high, or was he? He saw the doctor's slick black hair in a pointed widow's peak. The dark main shock swept back from the forehead, the silvery smooth glisten of the sidewalls in a pronounced *C* around the ears. Spit coagulated on the doctor's lower lip. His teeth were gray, and Zeb thought: I should kill this man.

From the front pocket of his jeans Zeb drew a gun, easily, fluidly, as if his pocket was substantial and made of silk. The gun was obnoxiously large, but Zeb's hand felt sure. He lifted and held the weapon high and read the print engraved on the stock: .38 Special. He lowered the gun and pointed it at the doctor's chest and the doctor smiled. The doctor pulled the gun forward and brought it close, compelled before being shot to read the words for himself: .44 Magnum this time. Nice, Zeb thought, and he let his arm come even. He breathed out, pulled his index finger gently and the gun banged and sent his hand to the ceiling, the shot like a small bomb in the hallway. The doctor smiled again. Zeb lay on the floor, a hole the size of a cereal dish in his own left chest, a star of red around the circumference, and people were running.

"She's gray," Sara said.

They were running down white tile floors with big-volumed words and the words were unwieldy and Zeb got caught in them while his wife was wheeled, white-sheeted between silver swinging doors. Before she disappeared he saw how hard her face had become, how the lines in it had gone dark and straight and the skin looked tight, almost iridescent.

He wasn't with her again until it was over. The white coats walked her down the hall and dropped her off with him in the lobby. They assured him the bleeding had stopped, her heart rate had come steady. She stood beside him, vacant, almost weightless. He put his arm around her. Everyone had gone. She leaned her head into his chest. He felt blank and dark.

He looked at his right hand, the gun stuck like an unwanted appendage there. His left hand was full of blood. He walked the hall and no one spoke to him. He had no hands. The tiles came to an end and he walked over the precipice and fell full and far before he rose with his arms in the shape of an eagle's wings, splendid and precise, his body streamlined and new, the body of a boy in an alley asleep between two dumpsters, a wedge of small stones piled against the windbreak his head makes.

From a hole in the half-world came a reverend—Mr. Reyes, the half-Cheyenne, half-white man he'd seen only once in the green hall of the clinic back in Lame Deer after the first miscarriage. His face, his words. "Son, this from God to your child." Into the silence. "I have made you. I will not forget you. Sing for joy." The great expanse of a deep gorge among high mountains, the closeness, the vastness of all things. In the black of morning he finds Sara's form curved into him, her back to his chest, her legs matched neatly to his. Her hair smelling of dry sweat, and faintly of lilac. How utterly I have failed you, he thinks. He kisses the back of her head and says, "You are my beloved." She clutches a braid of sweetgrass to her chest and he sees the plains to the straight edge of the alien world with nothing in between, the sun a dull white orb behind the gray sky. Caught in a crease on the horizon, a glow of light is the bright rim of all that lives and moves.

"They took her from me," she whispers. "She was gray."

The room is shadow. People never break free, he thinks.

The simple sound of a car on a dirt road eclipses the electric circuitry of the industrial machine and silences the speedwire of technology. Dawn is suddenly framed in the bedroom window.

He finds the shape of their bodies under the star quilt, senses the stillness, the proximity of their faces. He is home again. Born to this world. Shine. Early morning, April 4, his wife lies in bed beside him, holding something.

"Wake up, Z," she says. "You're here, with me."

On waking, he hears wheels on gravel as the car fades into the distance.

He is fully alive now and staring at Sara's face. In the light between them he sees the child. She is on her side, small, elongated, helpless, her form a tiny keepsake they carry like an amulet surrounded by the heart-shaped angles of their bodies, their legs and arms, as they face one another in the soft hope of their bed.

It is Sara's mouth that speaks the words, it is her body, the alluring movement of her hip beside him, and the way his hand must hold the curve of her ribs to know the breath that resides there, the rise and fall not of her whisper but of the engine from which her whisper moves. Not the pale cross of her collar-bones more reminiscent of Christ than Valentino's fine lines, but that down below the bones, the beating and drumming of the heart and the certainty from which her confidence lifts and opens the night. He sees the beginnings of her smile, then bright and turned to him, her eyes, pools in the wilderness he calls his own. Finally, he sees the ring, so insignificant, so lovely on the wounded hand. He places his hand under hers, and she turns her hand to hold his, the fingers small and warm in the grooves of his own. The imperfection is a grace to him, a strength he has needed all his life.

"Where are you?" he asks.

"I am with you," she answers.

In the sunshine he beholds his daughter's face, the sweet smell of vanilla quiet in her breathing, the sounds she makes as she coos and drifts sleepy in her mother's arms, and he sees that this then is the song to which every dream is tethered, a light infinite and sure, a divine light that gathers all hope in his hands, and he reaches out to his wife and cradles her head, and traces her lips with the tips of his fingers, and to them both before he sleeps he whispers, My darling. My love.

—for Jonathan Johnson

THE WAY HOME

SOME MILES WEST of Jimtown Bar, Nathan Bellastar traveled hard on a thin gravel road that divided the wheat fields. The wind was loud in the cab, and dust curled and billowed in his wake. Driving, he remembered what his mother said when he had failed again the very week his child was born. He'd been arrested in Colstrip for letting his truck roll through a stop sign and travel the sidewalk for fifty feet. "Admit it," she'd said when he'd made it home the next morning. "You're just a cheap drunk like all the rest." She was sitting in the recliner he'd bought for himself, in the living room of his own trailer, and she'd said it in front of his wife and newborn. She was supposed to be here to help with the child, but he'd counted it against her—the gray weight of her skin, her unwashed hair, the fat coil of her face—he had hated her.

Beneath the openness of sky and moon and stars, the gold of the fields lay dimly illumined. Here, when the day died, the heaviness was always the worst. He pictured a large, oblong stone lodged deep back in his chest cavity beneath his shoulder blades. The slope of his back felt rock hard. His ribcage had become constricted and he disliked the shallow breaths he had to take. Breathing shouldn't be something a man has to work at,

he thought. He reminded himself to forget his friends, the men
waiting for him up ahead. He could nearly taste the bite of the
alcohol in his mouth, the hot spiral in his throat as the whiskey went down. He tried to remember his daughter, the baby
smell of her breath, the way she touched at his eyes with her
tiny fingers. But as he sped onward the need in him outgrew
his will and rapidly he got to where he could hardly recall his
daughter's face. In the rearview mirror he found his own face
bony and thin.

EARLIER, JEDIDIAH had cut into him when they threw the last
bales of the evening. Jed was a big man with thick hands and a
pocked face, gritty at the hairline. A dirty ring lined the collar of
his denim shirt. "You gonna come with us tonight or not?" Jed
said. Nathan watched Jed's manner, the way he jerked each bale
from the ground as if he were in a fight. He noted this, but said
nothing and kept working.

"I figured as much," said Jed, and he stood and squinted at
Nathan. "You been pretty much cutting out on your friends
lately." Jed spit snuice on the ground.

Nathan kept hoisting bales while Jed stood waiting, staring
darkly at him. Nathan felt it and didn't like it, but he knew Jed
wouldn't understand. Jed would just undercut him like he had
before, slapping him on the back, shouting, "Come on! You got
time for one. A man deserves something for a day's work." And
Nathan would give in like a fool, like there was nothing but
straw in his spine.

Nathan turned his back to him now.

"Yeah," said Jed. "Just like I figured," and he spit again. He
muscled bales and said nothing, just grunted and stopped once
to spit out his chaw, then stepped in front of Nathan to grab
the last few bales and hurl them onto the stack.

Watching Jed drive off in his beat-up Ford sedan, Nathan

felt the burden begin in the upper part of his shoulders, then down and inward until it was embedded again, directly under the shoulder blades. The severity of the feeling made him wince. Immediately he desired to cover it over, dull it away with hard drinking. He'd heard others talk of phantom things like this, weird pains that came when you tried to stop. He forced himself to wait until the boys had all gone, Jed and the others, not just follow blindly as he desired. He wished the weight would die out, but it kept on.

Nathan noticed the line at the horizon, dark, distinct. He rubbed the pad of his thumb along the smoothness of his lips, a ritual that always commenced when he started a self-imposed drought. He knew he'd been touching his thumb to his lips all day now, like a kid that couldn't control himself. Hiding his hand in his pocket, he told himself to stop being such an idiot. He walked aimlessly for a time, half-inspecting the line of the bales, kicking or pushing at a few, but when he had straightened all he could, gassed and parked the machines along the south fence, and checked the northern gate, there was nothing left but to turn his truck to the road home. At first as he drove the dark sky had been clear, while off to the west an arm of sun remained, outstretched low and still on the land.

But as the sunlight gave way, clouds came in from the north and cloaked the earth and pushed back the stars. The land became bulky, hard to see but for the shoulders of the road and the earthen embankments that rose and fell from view almost before he noticed. Hardly distinguishable now, the track of the moon lay in the southern quadrant of the sky. Darkness had taken up the largest part of his surroundings, but in glimpses across open fields pale remnants of light pulled at the world's rim. As he drove, the headlights opened the night. Nathan tried to push his thoughts down. He knew the most difficult part lay ahead, over a rise and around one broad swell.

Down there the neon glow of Jimtown Bar was a weak pulse in the expanse of prairie. Descending the broad curve he lost sight of the bar for a time. He felt the pull of the engine, and heard the noise of it rapping out behind him. Then he rounded the hill and bearing down he saw Jimtown bright as bone. An ugly place, dark inside, lit up outside by the fluorescent bloom of the roadway sign. The building was a small raw square on the rez line, discolored, into which Indians and whites descended together, mostly Northern Cheyennes and some Crow, and in with them the white boys who worked the fields, or came out from Lame Deer. Last year a man had been knifed to death behind the building. Nathan and every man he worked with liked the feel of the place, always had. They're all inside, thought Nathan, laughing and drinking at a table just inside the door. Jed's cheeks would redden as he cackled, his large head would nod back to put another one down.

For a moment Nathan recognized how odd it was, how crazy in fact, that all this was so attractive to him. Then the notion died and he was caught again wanting to burn, wanting to throw off every resistance. The daughter he loved seemed distant, something faint, and far beyond his reach. He envisioned himself pulling into the parking lot, walking in the pseudolight of the neon sign as he hurried toward the door, his shirt half open, his eyes turned down. Thinking this way, his own face became foreign to him, the deep-set lines of his forehead, the tightening of his countenance. With his palm he tried to unfurrow it all, to push it up and back, but before he noticed, his hand was at his lips again, brushing at the shape of them, thumbing the smoothness there. Losing himself to the feel of it he knew the movement was no help. In the midst of it he was struck by the desire to press a bottle to his mouth and down liquor, as much of it as he could lay his hands on. He pounded his fists on the wheel and commanded himself aloud, "Right now. Knock it off!"

Back in early May he had come home late again and found
his wife asleep on the couch, tired from the pregnancy. He had
watched her for a moment, the way she lay on her side in one of
his T-shirts, her small body round and tight from the baby. He approached her and smoothed her hair from her face. She turned to
him. She kissed his mouth, and she asked him, "Nathan, will you
name our daughter?" These words. Even after they had cursed
each other when he called from the bar that night.

In a bent tone he asked her, "Why me?"

"Because," she said openly, "you're a good man. You're her
father, and I'd like it if you would."

Almost without will he said, "Okay." Face-to-face like this, she
could do that to him, call him to a ground he'd have never taken
alone. He carried her to the bedroom and wrapped her neatly
in the down comforter her mother had given them. Over the
covers he lay next to her and held her and gently pressed his
cheek to her face, feeling against his own face the bones of her
forehead, the circlet of bone around her eyes, and underlying her
eyes the cheekbones. When she had fallen asleep, he whispered,
"I'll be her father." And he knew the name he'd give.

IGNORING the bulky feel in his chest and back, the labor it
was to breathe, he set his face to the road and stepped the gas
to the floorboard. To avoid drawing his thumb to his lips he
consciously gripped the wheel in his fists. Quietly, but aloud, he
said his daughter's name—"Noel." At the sound of it something
increased in him, and as he drew near to Jimtown he kept the
pedal down. Neon flashed in the cab for a moment before it died
behind him. In the rearview mirror he watched it narrow and
fade, then disappear. Just like that, he thought, simpler than it
seemed. But long after the bar had passed he looked in the mirror, eyeing the road ahead only for a moment at a time.

More than ten miles on, the sky had opened and Nathan shut

off the headlights before turning on the dirt road that led to his
home. He entered the trailer and closed the door softly behind
him. Pausing, he rested his hands on the back of a metal folding
chair at the kitchen table. He heard the rhythm and the stillness
of his wife's breath, this with the breathing of his child, quiet
like the whisper of willows and wild rose.

He walked the hall and stopped at the open doorway, the
last door, the master bedroom. The moon was full in the room.
A slight breeze from the window touched him. A cedar chest
made by his wife's father was at the foot of the bed. In the bed,
his wife slept beneath the down coverlet, only the black veil of
her hair visible up near the headboard. Words came to him
that he'd heard her whisper on occasion when the babe slept
in her arms: "The garment of praise instead of the spirit of de-
spair." He thought he remembered her reading those words
somewhere. He loved the sound of them, the movement they
made in his mind.

Beside the window he saw his daughter's crib, the child asleep
within, and drawing near he stood over her. Hardly breathing, he
stared. He saw the line of her jaw, the small closed lids of her
eyes. She is so perfect, he thought, so fresh and new. The moon-
light is an angel in whose wings she breathes and sleeps. She was
no longer than his forearm, and when he reached down her head
fit in the palm of his hand. He smoothed her hair, then drew his
hand back and folded his arms over the railing.

Here he beheld her, and in the lovely way of her form he
found the echo of himself.

He went to the foot of the bed and folded his pants and shirt
and placed them in a small pile on the floor. In bed, he touched
his wife's arm and whispered as she slept, I'm grateful for you,
You are a good woman, I know a good woman, and as the last
words left his lips he drifted, sleeping.

★ ★ ★

IN THE NIGHT he woke and heard the child's breathing again, like a lost rhythm calling him. He got up and approached her crib, and from his place near the window, arms folded on the railing, he looked out. In the early light the line of the earth seemed a great distance away and barely visible, and there in the dim new world he saw everything: her tender form sleeping, his own faint reflection in the window, and out far the land, the stars, and water in between, the darkness and the dawn.

—for my grandfathers

THE MIRACLES
OF VINCENT VAN GOGH

THE SIMPLE TRUTH: John Sender believed in love. Thirty-three. Still single. Driven, too driven. So much head work, and such solitude, but now into his self-doubt, love. Real love. A love he could hardly believe after such drought, but yes, he believed. He'd even gone home to Montana and borrowed his long-dead grandfather's black Florsheim wing-tips from his recently dead grandmother's bedroom closet, and from her bureau the diamond ring she'd kept through two foreign wars—his mom wanted him to have it—the ring he'd be giving to his bride.

Only he hadn't much spoken with his bride yet.

He pressed his hands down on the desk, flattening them, staring. Big boned, rough. Late night; everyone gone. Alone again. The day had been difficult, another without tone or hue, loans drawn up, rates unsecured or secured, monies meted out. Awkward, the bones of a hand, beautiful in their way. His were like his father's, not afraid of work. Strong like his father's too, but meek with women.

He had thought he might just stick to horses; they calmed him every bit as much as he calmed them, the kind-spirited ones, the wild ones too, like bolts of lightning he could get a heel into and fight. He missed it, breaking for Dad and the neighbors. That, and all the rodeoing he'd done.

Spooked since he could remember, he felt like a fool on every date he'd been on, which was few. Tall man: six feet five, wired tight. Bridge of the nose bony as a crowbar, broken on a fence in Flagstaff. Rodeo docs always salty, that one had laid him flat on the ground, shoved two metal rods up his nose and got on top of him, then jerked the rods hard. The sound was unnatural, the pain like a landslide in his brain. Straightened things out but left a crude notch. Too tall for saddle broncs the doc said, but he'd made do.

Hard-nosed, his dad said when he saw the nose.

Keeps the women away, John answered, and they chuckled.

But John was better looking than he gave himself credit for. Shoulder-length black hair, black enough it had a blue sheen, drawn back, crowlike. Vivid eyes. Bold features. Big. Just quiet with women. He put his hands through his hair. Easier to see couples enter his office hoping to secure something . . . a loan, a home. The men were anomalies. Their wives called them husband, or hubby, or honey—or silent, said nothing. The men didn't know what they had, John thought. When it came to love, they should realize what they borrow is a woman: you borrow her from her family, from her mother and father, and mostly from God.

John's daily business was loans. Tailored suit and silk tie. Late again, after dark, he needed to finish the paperwork and get home. Odd, he thought. Vicarious living or some kind of narrow foresight. No cowboy hat, no boots, he felt at odds with himself. A rodeo scholarship and a BA in English from the University of Montana, then three years on the circuit and an MBA along with a smattering of additional graduate work in philosophy from Seattle University. He'd been in loans now nearly a decade, and until he met Samantha everything had seemed caught in a time strange to him, and uglified. Hollow, missing the land and sky. The ranch. Mom and Dad by themselves and him a corporate hired hand, trapped like a pawn in some large thoughtless efficiency, all take, no give. To borrow implied not only responsibility but culpability. But men were made mostly of emptiness, he thought, palpable, burdensome.

And of the men who borrowed?

Their lives, like his, were made as much of confusion as clarity, edging toward death but wanting life, poised on the tipping point between dark and light. Tangibly they ranged the border between self-sabotage and a new country of grace, and it worried him, the threshold over which a man must pass, the crucible. He worried about them, and yet how easily he forgot them.

THE FORGOTTEN, two among many.

Sean Baden. Elias Pretty Horse.

Two he'd forgotten. Two who had forgotten him. He'd seen them in the beginning, way back when, and these days it was true, life so hectic, so recessed and depressed, no one felt compelled to remember, though even slight remembering might have meant help, and remembering well might have meant salvation. Men, dumb as animals, but like angels, majestic. Born into foolishness. Into love awakened. Unknowingly they willed themselves to succeed or die.

JOHN PLACED A STACK of loans in the processor's in-box.

Past midnight locking the office door his hands felt very cold. He hoped beyond fear she'd come to like him but he had to laugh at himself, everything so unlikely still. He'd only been in her close proximity once, but as he merged onto I-5 for the forty-minute commute from downtown he pushed the ring over his right pinkie finger, a simple solitaire, firm hand at twelve o'clock, and watched the glow through the windshield, subdued

usually but in the direct light of oncoming vehicles the stone
a tiny torch of white, gold, and vermilion. He envisioned placing the ring on her slight hand, smiling into her eyes, receiving
from her the smile she'd give. He dreamed of trips back home
to Montana, where he drove Going to the Sun Road in Glacier,
hiked the lakes region from Hidden Lake at Logan Pass, to
Avalanche Lake and Two Medicine. He'd teach her to fly-fish.
He'd make small bright fires under wide skies on nights that
would deepen from light to dark blue then black as black silk,
silver points like fine sand from east to west, the Milky Way an
arm of clustered stars overhead. The Summer Triangle. Cygnus
the Swan. Vega, Altair, Albireo. In the western night they'd shine,
he and she like satellites.

That night in bed, he held his hands over his chest and stared
at the ceiling. Chill air, down comforter his mother gave him a
Christmas ago. The reasons men borrowed were simple, and not
so simple. They borrowed what they felt they needed, and not
just from him, from everyone, and not just money, they borrowed
everything. He thought about the real needs: a job, sex, marriage?
They borrowed against their line of credit, cash, jewels, furniture,
paintings, vintage guitars, home theaters, cars. A house, a home.
They borrowed money even to buy their own beds. In isolation
it was nothing but combined it meant great debt, depending on
who borrowed what, and for how much, and when.

SEAN BADEN borrowed his father's Bible.

JOHN HAD TO admit he felt low in Seattle, real low away from
home, boxed in by granite and glass, and the rain, no range or
visibility, no sky, and out among the millions he'd nearly given
up hope. It wasn't the flats near Rock Springs where you could
ride for miles and never see a soul and never feel alone. Here,
you hit people constantly, bumped them on the sidewalk or in

a grocery line, touching and being touched and never knowing anyone, you couldn't get away from the sheer mass even if you wanted to; it made you feel bad.

Yet here he'd found her.

He stared at the ceiling. His hands wouldn't warm up.

TO WIN WOMEN men put on an attitude of cleanliness, clipped nails, and shaved faces, sideburns like little battle-axes, a soul patch below the lower lip or a thin goatee, lines of facial hair crisp, hard, geometric, glistening. They borrowed colognes like engines of desire: Fahrenheit, Body Heat, Obsession. Beneath the surface of the world and over the surface and above it the mystery moved, granting men the will to find someone, some men by purpose or chance possessing more push than others, men filled or being filled of hope or hopelessness, men satiated, men left wanting.

ELIAS PRETTY HORSE, Assiniboine-Sioux with a fine-boned face and eyes like a storm, borrowed his father's beaded drum mallet and placed it on the corner of his desk at Northwest Farm and Implement. Slender, he was a runner, holder of high school records in the mile and two-mile. He set the ivory bridal teeth of an elk on either side of the mallet to remind him work, and women, were like singing, like pealing wild riffs from a high vocal front the same way a man cut calves from the herd for branding. The hard beats that sounded from the drum came like blood, the thrumming and singing wholly untame. Brothers. His brothers came from everywhere. The group in Seattle had singers from five nations.

IN AMERICA, if a man was so inclined he borrowed the will to find a woman. He borrowed velocity, projection, and pretense—he borrowed need. The need to be. The need to be seen. He borrowed emotion, physicality, tenacity, trouble. Undoubtedly each

one had it, elegant but unrefined, the mystery of manhood un-
diluted and unbridled—the inner inferno that was his sex. Made
equally of darkness and light, they were men. They were brash
and frail, and married.

AND JOHN SENDER, alone. On free fall in the apartment, linear, solid, spare. Unable to sleep he moved from the bed to the
kitchen, drank a glass of milk, went to the leather reading chair,
and stared at the window. Odd reflection: long white body,
white T-shirt, white underwear, skin like alabaster. He leaned
and took an old issue of *Montana Quarterly* from the rack beside
him. He read an article on a wolverine researchers collared that
crossed nine mountain ranges in forty-two days. He fell asleep
in the chair. He woke, stumbled back to bed. Night sifting the
sediment of dreams. Dark animal, solitary, full of speed. Light.
Morning. Glass of water. Toast. No TV, no radio. No sound.
Driving I-5 to work he lifted from the heart pocket of his suit
coat the pen Samantha had given him that first chance meeting. He thought of her holding the pen, a blue ballpoint made
of inexpensive metal alloy, pens the bank gave out. He'd seen
her in the lobby after work, seated, writing a memo, a note to
a friend, or perhaps her mother, left-handed—a note to him, he
liked to imagine—her clear nail polish and French manicure, the
pale half-spheres at the base of her fingernails like small suns
touched to the ocean of her skin. It was sudden: he had desired
her more than anything.

Awful, the anxiety he had over his voice being too boyish, his
face too pale and hands too hard. He sat down next to her. "Can
I borrow your pen?" he said.

"Sure," she said, handing it to him. "Keep it." She slipped her
fingers into her purse and drew forth an identical pen.

"Handy," he said. His hands were not only cold but sweating.
She smiled.

He managed a few awkward questions. She grew up in Bellingham. She mentioned her family, her mom, studies, work. She looked right at him, not away.

He lost himself.

"Can I take you to dinner?" he said.

"What?" she replied.

"Sorry," he said.

He's country, she thought. She didn't dislike him.

His hands flushed with sweat again, so he waved at her and turned to go and she smiled, and he was astonished at how much her smile delighted him. Down the hall, when she couldn't see, he slapped his hands together, covered his mouth, and muffled a slight whoop. She hadn't even said yes. Still, he thought perhaps the top of his head was on fire.

THE RING felt like a small star in his pocket. Through the elevator doors, passing her floor, the third, going to his, the fifth, he was afraid. The first time on a saddle bronc was no different: exhilaration, and horror. Glad he'd had the buck rein his dad bought for him secondhand, worn in and comfortable, if blackened. Single thick rope, awkward, tricky as a rattlesnake. He'd lost it when the horse went rump high straight out of the chute, launching him head first into the dirt. Still, the buck rein was the only help; tiny saddle and his own fatal balance no good to him at all. Bruised shoulder, and dirt in the nose and teeth for a week. Not a natural by any means, but he could work. It took seven rodeos to complete his first real ride and when it came, it unhooked him good. Digging spurs, arm high, horse a force of nature below, and John a bright dream above. The classic event of rodeo, skill and finesse over straight strength. He'd held the whole eight seconds, bounced and landed on his feet full of spit and fire. Cheer from the small-town crowd. Town called Rosebud, dust bowl, eastern Montana. Fatherless Child was her name, eleven-hundred-pound fighter he never saw again. Still loved that horse.

Loved all the horses he'd ridden. Metal chute, knees high-rails above the shoulders. The crowd, the gate pullers, the pickup men. Grit in the glove, horse's back hard as stone; muscle it down ready. Knees up, spurs down, chute gate flung wide and animal and man sprung out clean and tight and wild. Tossed on a string, close to tetherless, horse like white lightning, free hand touching sky, punching, pulling, power in the hand of fear, and fear in the gut, and below fear tenderness, and deeper down, down deep love.

OFF THE ELEVATOR, John walked the hall and saw the men in their cubicles and felt convinced that every man in the fortified world wanted an answer to the loneliness, an answer that might help him set his world aright.

SEAN BADEN in a rancher east of the city. His smiling wife.

ELIAS PRETTY HORSE, generous and strong hearted, a long-distance runner. A hard worker. He cherished his mother despite her hard-lived life. He cherished his Assiniboine wife, Josefine. Her strong legs and bold front-forward posture. A woman made like rivers and boulders.

Townhouse on the outskirts of Auburn.

JOHN LOVED the kindness and complexity, the eccentricity. Because of Samantha it seemed he could love everything, the arc of his thoughts enhanced like blown glass. Now he found everyone beautiful, like works of art, something sacred he should give his life for. He remembered Van Gogh: the words standing as if written in light: *the greatest work of art is to love someone.* He could give Samantha his whole life, he knew he could.

Still, it's hard to stop thoughts, he thought, especially the will to fail . . . or how the mind so quickly condemns. He needed courage for what he was about to do. He walked back to his desk and stared at his screensaver, panorama of Glacier's mountains shouldering the blue of Hidden Lake. He wanted to make a life with her. He felt sick. He sent the first in a collection of small bright e-mails. Then came a phone call, followed by a meeting in the third-floor lounge. A shared lunch at week's end and a week later the first real date: at Anthony's Seaport over the water.

She asked of his schooling, his interests, religion, work, his dreams. She scared him, very much. But he felt vital in her presence. Stunning, her chestnut hair and high-boned face. He wasn't all business, she was glad, and told him so, intrigued with his upbringing, his background in English and philosophy. For his part she reminded him of the great poets: terrifying, exact.

Three months later, she put him on the spot.

"You ready for me?" she said.

He looked at his shoes, his grandfather's shoes.

"I think so," he said. But what was the lineup he'd drawn in Reno? It wasn't the animals with menacing names like Hell's Fire, or Kitchen-of-the-Damned, or Homicidal Tendencies that got you, it was the playful-named ones like Honey-Do, or Conjunction Junction. Hell's Fire and HT were nothing. Honey-Do nearly broke his neck.

Even the mean ones he loved, but he wasn't dumb; you could get kicked in the head by something you loved, and often it took a lot to avoid it. On the circuit you had to be careful, but with abandon. Supervigilant, half-crazed. Everything so large-scale at the big rodeos—Oklahoma City, Cheyenne, Denver, Provo, Sacramento. No more eleven-hundred-pounders, it was thirteen or more, fifteen hundred sometimes, horse blowing snot in the chute, white-eyed, fast, and powerful, and leap like a gymnast. Roads, long black lines gray at the edges, hard driving, hard riding. He'd broken thirty bones, mostly fingers and other hand bones, plus ribs; he'd cracked a collarbone too, fractured his right scapula, and in a rodeo in Miles City broken his jawbone. Had his face wired up. Ate through a straw for months.

He looked at the shoes. The first day he'd tried them on he found a sheen of dried blood on the shell of the left one. He was twenty-three, just weeks after his grandfather's funeral. Back then it took no energy, his mind didn't dwell; he had licked his thumb and removed the stain. He wore the shoes for an hour or two, then put them back in Grandma and Grandpa's closet. But now he thought darkly of his grandpa without wanting to. Tough old man who rarely talked. Real down, John thought, ending it on a Sunday, body laid out behind the barn, head slung back and to the side. He remembered the slender barrel of the .270 flat on the grass. Then Grandma years later, but not violent, dignified, even with Grandpa still a big hole in everything.

John looked at Samantha. His eyes were teary.

Be ready, John's dad had always told him, and John knew she'd make him step up the same way a bronc made a man reach, spur from the shoulder down, drop-swing motion, shoulder to ribwork, untempered, but rhythmic like a drum.

Alone in the high country he'd stop and lay his head on his horse's neck, Black, or Charlie, the two his dad still kept for him back home, Black an Arabian cross, high in the legs and narrow face, and Charlie an old palomino quarter horse. The sweet grass smell of the coat, breathing in, exhaling—it brought him back from any distance.

EVERY MAN BORROWED. He borrowed things both common and strange, things cold like cash, or things more ultimate, like charisma and concern, or below these, and more virile—more core—anger, distance, deviance.

A man not only borrowed money, he borrowed the skills of

other men. He borrowed, or bought with borrowed money as he was able, talent at carpentry and handiwork, his neighbor's hammer, his band saw, his understanding of power panels and pilot lights, his wrench, his tool belt, his box of screws, nuts, nails. He borrowed ideas, attitudes, actions. Always, he borrowed more than he knew.

BACK IN Wolf Point Elias Pretty Horse borrowed his grand-mother's beaded coin purse to place on his desk with his father's drum beater and the elk's eyeteeth.

SEAN BADEN borrowed time, evenings, to read his father's Bible. Passages about Christ humbling himself, about the Son of God not considering equality with God a thing to be grasped, but humbling himself, taking the form of a man. Sean's wife, the floor manager for Nordstrom's in women's shoes, still liked him.

Not for long, Sean thought.

He felt edgy in the head; he hated himself; he wanted sex; and not from her.

HOUSED IN THE FACE of the men who came to John for money, there was more than their women bargained for. The truth of each man was that he borrowed sexual greed and hun-ger, emptiness and voracious hunger . . . thoughts, conversa-tions, chatrooms, disloyalty . . . night silence, computer time, porn, extreme porn. Men opaque and secretive who borrowed what their fathers borrowed before them, the emotionless vessel of their own habits, the way their wives hated them—the hatred men engendered.

And yet, for all their ugliness, still they borrowed love.

Not merely disillusionment or desperation, they borrowed listening, and quietness, loveliness. They borrowed the urge that sent them in the evening walking with their wives, or brought them to the table, a deck of cards, a conversation, songs the marriage shared, whispers. They borrowed greetings at the door, good-byes. They borrowed dancing. They borrowed the stars their eyes beheld, the hopes that bore them up.

They were beautiful. They were terrible.

They tried everything, but everything was often not enough and before love died they looked fiercely at the future and borrowed the illusion of love's permanence, and oh how her body had leaned into him, and oh how she had loved his willing heart, and each man remembered in his bitterness how once his kiss was her secret exultation, and how now when he looked he saw he repulsed her, and in the end, no matter a man's makeup, when love waned he went from her like a dog with his tail between his legs, and trying still, men worked more and borrowed more, borrowed more money, borrowed their fathers' shovels and backhoes, they dug trenches in new backyards, placed sprinkler systems and fences, some fences higher than others, and deeper the trenches, and each wife, openly or secretly, despised her man for selling her out.

ELIAS PRETTY HORSE witnessed two deaths in his family during his first year in high school at Wolf Point, both cousins, one male, one female. They'd been close to him nearly from birth, children of his uncles' families. Paulina Pretty Horse took a cocktail of her mother's prescriptions, muscle relaxants, Thorazine, and Zoloft. She fell asleep and stopped her heart. Griffith Dogchild, drunk, drove his brother's motorcycle into the concrete wall of a highway overpass at 2:00 a.m. after a kegger in the Missouri Breaks. Land like a wrinkled old blanket. The bike a pillar of flame when it struck.

Elias saw his own father drag his mother down a flight of stairs by her hair, breaking her sternum, dislocating her right shoulder. To counter the undertow he'd run stoic and mostly silent all through high school, then gone to Fort Peck Community College for two years and on to a scholarship at Montana State, where he graduated with honors and a bachelor's degree in public relations. He vowed he'd escape, get away from the craziness. Live as he was meant to live.

He landed an internship with Montana Feed and Co., a ranch supply operation in Missoula, and when they hired him on it took him nearly no time to increase the company's market range from Montana to Wyoming and North and South Dakota. At age twenty-five, a headhunter tagged him for a lead manager position at Northwest Farm and Implement in Seattle. He'd always thought of his wife as a better person than he, more alive, more ready to give and forgive. He'd go where she called. A light, he thought, to lead him. A fire that made him burn like he was fuel. She'd been with him all the way from Wolf Point to Fort Peck and on to Bozeman. She didn't know quite everything of his past, and he too was blind to much of hers. From age eleven to fifteen an aunt named Juniper molested him, and for her part she'd suffered indignities she kept silent.

She hadn't wanted to go to Seattle.

They'd gone to Seattle anyway.

SEAN BADEN, THE CHRISTIAN worker, was a poor student. When he was young he borrowed his sister's class notes and proceeded to fail his freshman year in high school twice. He might have had a learning disability, but his father said God is in control and refused his daughter's wish to get Sean professional help. The school, being fundamentalist, Christian, and private, said the same, and Sean, having suffered the loss of his mother at age eight, did not go against his father's wishes. At sixteen he flunked out of school, never having passed ninth grade. At eighteen he discovered massage parlors and hand jobs. At twenty he was a delivery man for a food services company that shipped candy throughout the Northwest. On his third overnight trip, on a stop just outside Boise, he lost his virginity with a small-town prostitute. Her skin was cold and she didn't speak. She kept her face to the wall. He hated himself. At twenty-three he got his GED, moved to Portland and began work in construction. He met Sarah at a nice church, nondenominational with good worship, and fell in love. By now he'd received more than one hundred hand jobs and had sex with twenty-seven prostitutes. He vowed to stop. He was successful until the night after he and Sarah were engaged, when he left his apartment, walked ten blocks to Sal's Therapeutic Massage, and was masturbated by a short sixteen-year-old Asian girl named Louise.

MEN BORROWED compulsion, fear, disaster, desire.

THE NEXT DAY Sean told Sarah everything, and she left him.
    Three days later she called and said she'd still marry him but he had to go to counseling. He agreed and for three months they went twice weekly to see their pastor. On their wedding day Sean sang a song and Sarah cried. On their wedding night Sean cried. He felt like a virgin again. It took him six years to get a four-year Bible degree from Western Christian, a small private college in Vancouver, Washington. Sarah read his textbooks aloud and every night he taped her voice, stream of mercy, and listened and relistened until he knew the material. He was accepted for a position with Campus Crusade and successfully raised the required ninety percent of his support goal (a salary of twenty-five thousand per year from family, friends, and strangers giving monthly or one-time gifts). He reported to headquarters in San Bernardino, California, with Sarah for eight weeks of training after which he was assigned to the University of Washington to lead worship—he had a strong tenor voice—and be in charge of evangelism for the Crusade ministry there. Clean, nearly debtless,

two used cars bought with cash—a loan with no points was easy and way back, when they had walked away from John Sender's office holding hands, they'd walked away happy, their faces lit like lanterns.

THE MEN OF THE NATION, by and large, if they were married more than seven years, wore a tough face, a grimace at how it had happened to them as it seemed to happen to everyone—sex no longer easy, their wives despised them, the grace of a smile false or forgotten.

Men borrowed the will to forget their wives.

Men wandered and fantasized, they glazed their eyes with found porn.

They spoke to other women, they slept with them.

SEATTLE, THE SUN hidden. John hadn't slept much.

He was in his office at 7:40 a.m. when he raised the receiver.

"Can we meet?"

"Sure."

When he greeted her he kissed her cheek and she smiled. She sat with one leg crossed over the other, tapestry skirt, light lavender blouse, her trim upper body forward some, her hands in her lap.

He looked out the window and breathed and tried to calm himself. He thought of pearl button shirts, three of them in a plastic container among the battlewares he'd carried on the road, the big canvas bag, the halter and halter strap, flank strap, buck rein, dulled spurs with rolling rowels, padded leather riding vest, bronc saddle in the floor space of the passenger side (lightweight, no horn), immaculate Stetson (black, felt) atop his head and beside him on the bench a simple straw cowboy hat, black-banded, twelve bucks at Kmart, no helmet, never liked helmets.

Her face looked pained.

"What's wrong?" he said.

"Nothing," she replied.

Something's wrong, he thought.

He tried to look at her without looking away. "Are you okay?" he said.

"Fine," she said.

She touched his arm.

Her hand light as a swift or mountain swallow.

He took her fingers in his. His hand started sweating. He tried to let go but she held on and looked into his eyes.

"Are you scared?" she said.

"Down to my boots," he said.

IN NOVEMBER he met her mother at their home on Mercer and by January he set a surprise trip and drove Samantha to Spokane, where they boarded the Amtrak Empire Builder and went by train north deep into Montana along the Hi-Line. He'd been dreaming of rodeo, big horses, sorrels and grays, blacks, massive crossbred pintos, paints, big roughstock from Texas, and him hat in hand and arm flying as he countered the arch-kicks and cut the leans. When they arrived at the station it was after sundown and cold. His mother and father greeted them, laughing, embracing them both, and they rode together into the fields for miles until they came upon a house, spare, with two outbuildings, and beyond it the long flat that bordered the Rocky Mountain front.

Three months earlier, John had called and asked if he could borrow Grandpa's two-person open carriage and at that request his father had brushed it up and set it with runners for winter. John's mother was more direct; she adorned the sleigh with ribbons and bows and small delicate bells, silvery, starlike.

In the dark of morning his father drew the carriage to the front door of the ranch house leading a large gray workhorse named Felicity, a family favorite, utterly gentle. John was in the old twin bed, the night black and formless around his face. Samantha was in the guest room, a room set west toward broad fields of snow and the expanse of range John's father owned, and farther on, the sheer uplift of mountains. John hadn't heard his dad go out, it was the familiar sounds that woke him: the tamp of hooves on fresh snow, the easy breath of the horse. He heard the glide of the runners on new wax, a slight shimmer of bells. They had coffee and cinnamon rolls with Mom and Dad in the kitchen. Samantha was effervescent, and unaware. John bundled her himself and she said, "How nice of you," and, "Thank you."

To her delight he lifted her in his arms and carried her out the front door to the sleigh. When she saw it she gasped, and looked at John, and buried her face in his coat. Her tears quieted him, and he drove her two miles in the half-dark to Deer Creek, cold air crisp and high in their lungs, snow covering the land to the east on a blue-white arc to the end of it all. From a rise of land they watched the sun emerge and fire the world and John held her hand and asked her to marry him.

WHAT MEN BORROWED varied based on income, based on instant gratification or inflated need, based on how all-consuming their habits might be. In addition to the money to pay for homes, appliances, landscaping, toys like boats, motorcycles, ATVs, they borrowed things they wished they hadn't. From the dull look in their fathers' eyes they borrowed the pain that resided there.

IN SEATTLE, for Elias Pretty Horse days became nights, and nights seemed void of light. Past midnight in Bozeman he'd stood on the edge of a canyon in the Spanish Peaks and raised his hands to the sky and shouted with all his gusto—the stars burned like candles, vast, uncountable, a glittering field that whirled overhead and made him feel small and great at once, a fancy dance, he thought. The embers of a lunar fire bright gold in the darkness. He'd won an important race that day. He felt he belonged. So he yelled the only blessing he knew, the Sioux word for thank you: Pee-la-mah-yah-yea! Pee-la-mah-yah-yea! He'd fallen to his knees then and said again, Thank you. It is good. You are very good. He didn't know if he was speaking of mother or father or spirit. He spoke to the sky. All my relations, he thought. I love you.

But after only two years in Seattle his wife seemed distant and he thought she might have already had three affairs, two with Muckleshoot men they'd met at the casino, the last with a Coeur D'Alene she came across at the farmers' market in Ballard. For his part Elias had lied to her more times than he cared to count, breaking every promise he'd made in their quiet Catholic wedding. A simple unfortunate progression—(a) lie and tell her you're going to get some milk, (b) slip into the black overhang of one hip white joint or another, (c) talk sweet and get a white girl drunk, (d) get drunk yourself and follow her home.

MEN WORKED ON borrowed time.
Little in the way of wisdom.

JOHN HOPED the best for people.
He and Samantha spoke tentatively, of life and the future, and likely because they weren't having any, they avoided talk of sex.
John was degrading himself to her image, using fantasy, trying to think only of Samantha. When he felt unable to resist he used porn, in which case he could not think of Samantha, or he could only think of her head on someone else's body.

WITHOUT FORETHOUGHT men borrowed things that might put them in good stead with women. They borrowed their father's gait, his manner of walking, the tones he used when he wanted his wife, the readiness. They borrowed his cool facial expression, the way he sat with one leg crossed over the other, forming a triangle between his legs, or kicked back, hands interlocked behind the head, legs crossed at the ankles. They also borrowed his rigid brow and manic intention, the speed at which he could do harm.

IN YEAR THREE the wife of Elias Pretty Horse left him. He was half-awake in the dark of their bed when Josefine kissed his cheek and said, "I'm going back to Wolf Point."

WHEN MEN GOT HOME from work, all of them borrowed, when supplies were low, against their wives' patience, their favorite foods, the last of the brownies, the final cookie, the last drink of milk, the remnant of cereal in the box, and each of them, when he was lazy or couldn't find his own, borrowed his wife's toothbrush, and when she was in the bathroom vocalizing, criticizing, he took her pillow to spite her, he took her side of the bed. Marriage was made of perception and defense, apathy, absence, contempt.

SEAN BADEN BORROWED money from his father three times in four years to help with hospital costs for the three daughters born to him and Sarah: Ruth, Hagar, Tamar. The Campus Crusade ministry at the University of Washington was filled with Holy Spirit fire. Sean's voice, throaty and bold, drew in close to one thousand students every Friday night. After one such Friday night he borrowed twenty dollars from his director, thinking he'd use it to take a couple of new converts for a burger and a coke. Except for relieving himself with porn, he'd been clean for some time. When the students said they couldn't go, Sean drove to the city center, parked his car, and went walking. He turned toward the white light of an open door, entered an adult bookstore, and watched a peep show for five dollars. Outside, a block farther on he spoke to a prostitute, walked with her into an alley, and paid her fifteen dollars to give him a blow job.

TO INCREASE their livelihood, to better their future, men borrowed whatever they could.

At night in the subtle glow from the dashlights, John remembered their faces and quirky mannerisms, their strange ways and enigmatic lives. He was getting better at defining them, not so rose colored. Men too neat, too tidy, or the dirty ones, unkempt, careless. These, and all the variations in between. He remembered their eyes, subsumed in small houses of flesh and bone, men who needed so much, some with hard mouths and slate faces eyeing their wives with menace or loathing, haughtiness, horror, and hate—and on the other side of the divide the ones he hoped to emulate. Considerate, quick to listen. Again he checked himself, he didn't understand anything about anyone. Even trying to understand himself seemed absurd.

But marriage, he thought. Marriage! He could hardly keep from shouting out loud. The truck wheels humming, he pictured himself walking with her in the high mountains, snowshoeing over an opaque world where trees stood flocked in white and the sky was a window on heaven, robin's egg blue and cloudless. They'd make their way to his grandfather's cabin, a well-appointed A-frame, and work together making things ready. John would clear a space on the tin roof to the cellar and put quarters out like his grandfather taught him. They'd build a fire in the woodstove and fill the kettle for tea, and while the house warmed they'd gather the quarters hot from the sun to warm their hands. He'd touch her face then and he would not be afraid.

The house would come alive with heat and they'd stand side by side and look out through the picture window that faced south where the blanketed land became incandescent at dusk and the sky's velvet was shattered by stars. Their children would sleep soundly, he thought, and wake fearless in the world. In the night he'd find her pressing her face to his, speaking kindness and goodwill, and there on the threshold of sleep he'd say, I believe in you, and from his lips would rise tender words in the darkness: You will be clothed with joy and brought forth with peace.

MEN BORROWED DIGNITY or they borrowed shame. Sean Baden locked himself in his bathroom for three days after he'd had sex twice in one night with two different prostitutes for forty dollars apiece, cold bodies, slack faces. His wife knew nothing and spent most of that time crying outside the bathroom door as she tried to call him out. She didn't tell the Crusade director or the director's wife. She didn't tell anyone. Their two oldest were with her parents for the week. She had Tamar with her. Sean lay on the bathroom floor on his side of the door, cheekbone to cold tile, wishing he could become that hard, like stone, unknowing, unknowable, unable to hurt or do hurt, unable to harm.

Opening the door and stepping over her, he left the bathroom for one hour and bought a ten-foot coil of rope from True Value Hardware in the U District. As he reentered the house he hid the purchase under his polo dress shirt and returned to the bathroom and closed and locked the door again. He felt capable of nothing. The rope was half-inch nylon boating rope, smooth and flexible. He didn't acknowledge Sarah anymore, or her pleas. She'd made a bed for herself and Tamar and he heard them breathing, the sounds subtle as soft harmonies. They didn't need him. They needed each other. He'd have the water running hard a good while before he did it. Past midnight he heard a loud knock on the door. Please, his wife said, talk to Tommy. Tommy Vigil was a youth pastor in Dallas, Texas. Sean and Tommy had taken the first two summers of Crusade courses together. Miles away, Sean thought. He cracked the door; he didn't look at Sarah. She placed the phone in on the bathroom floor. He pulled the door shut. On the other side she was seated cross-legged, listening. The child slept in her arms. She prayed.

The first sentence Tommy spoke was, "You're having sex with prostitutes again, aren't you?"

"Yes," Sean said, and his chin quivered.

He opened the door and sat down next to Sarah and the child. His tongue felt thick. He handed her the phone. "Sean has something to tell you," Tommy said. She put the receiver faceup on the carpet between them. Crying, he told her everything.

This time they went further, taking six years to gain back what they'd lost. Him working odd jobs, carpentry, road work, sand and gravel. Inpatient. Outpatient. Six years of counseling, mentoring, sponsors, recovery, self-reflection, vulnerability, responsibility; seeking to be pure, hoping to be. In year seven there was a public laying on of hands when he was reinstated as worship leader at the University of Washington. Same Crusade director, new flights of students, Sean was afraid and praying for courage. At night in his study working out the chord progression to a song called "I Will Sing of Your Love Forever," he paused, thinking. From the kitchen he overheard his wife on the phone talking to a friend. He's beautiful, his wife said. He's beautiful now. And Sean felt beautiful, and believed he might be beautiful forever.

DAILY, JOHN WATCHED men walk through the door and borrow against the future.

Borrowing from unseen places, from family and friends, from loved ones or strangers, they borrowed and were broken. They were broken; they were healed.

Many men fail, John thought, but some succeed.

* * *

BY YEAR FOUR in Seattle, Elias Pretty Horse was heading steadily downhill. He hadn't run for two years. He didn't sing anymore. And when once in the corner of his closet he found an empty jewel case of his Seattle drum group he decided not to return to work. He gained weight. Called himself pig. Lost his job. He needed to get on his feet. He hocked his dad's drum mallet, his grandmother's coin purse. He spent the money on fumes. He lay in bed morning to night for three months, but on a day in December under winter rain and bleak skies he rose from his stupor, stood outside on the balcony of the master bedroom in his townhouse, and called his dad. Elias asked his father if he could borrow some money. His father wired him the necessary amount and they met the next day at the airport in Great Falls.

By early evening Elias was home.

His mother prayed over him, he slept eleven hours, woke at dawn and started running again.

The next day he saw Josefine outside the Boys and Girls Club. He parked his father's truck and got out and when he approached she walked directly to him, held his hands, and said, "I'm glad you're here."

"I need to get right," he said. "I'm all wrong."

"You're here," she said, touching his face. "You're here now," and when she brought him close and kissed his forehead he sobbed in her arms.

AT NOON on a bright day in the city, a Saturday, John drove his truck to the modern cathedral in Edmonds. He glanced in the rearview mirror at his dad in the off-white Chevy Monte Carlo, his mom next to his dad on the bench seat, Dad's arm around Mom.

What we borrow who can repay? John thought.

He entered the wide wood doors of the church on the corner of Olympic and Pearl. He wore his grandfather's wingtips polished bright black. Next to his heart in the silk-lined pocket of the tuxedo, he kept the ring in its velvet box. He'd be giving it to Samantha's nephew, receiving it back in front of five hundred witnesses, and placing it on her finger.

Samantha heard him come in. She cracked the dressing room door. He hadn't seen her. She watched him move across the foyer into the sanctuary. At the head of the aisle he turned and looked back. He faced her directly. He still hadn't seen her. She loved his face, strong man looking out at the world. The skin was brazen, broken nose, pale eyes.

He turned and walked resolutely down the aisle.

With all his faith he'd say it to her out loud in front of everyone.

Say it with all his tenderness, all his love.

I do, I will.

PUBLICATION ACKNOWLEDGMENTS

The stories in this collection appeared in the following magazines: "How We Fall" in *Montana Quarterly* (Spring 2009), nominated for *Best American Short Stories* by editor Megan Ault Regnerus, winner of the *Pacific Northwest Inlander* Award for Fiction, and selected as a notable story in *Best American Nonrequired Reading* (2010); "The Great Divide" in *McSweeney's* (issue 12, lead story 2003), nominated for a Pushcart Prize by Dave Eggers and Eli Horowitz, nominated for *Best New American Voices* by faculty of the Inland Northwest Center for Writers MFA program at Eastern Washington University, and selected for the best of *McSweeney's* anthology *The Better of McSweeney's, vol. 2* (Spring 2010); "Three from Montana" in *Big Sky Journal* (Winter 2005); "Rodin's *The Hand of God*," winner of the *Crab Creek Review* Fiction Prize (Summer 2009); "When We Rise" in *Aethlon* (Fall 2005); "Mrs. Secrest" in *Narrative* (Winter 2005); "In the Half-Light" in *Talking River Review* (Winter 2005); "The Dark between Them" in *StoryQuarterly* (issue 41, 2004); "The Way Home" in *South Dakota Review* (Fall 2001); "The Miracles of Vincent van Gogh," selected by David James Duncan as the winner of the *Ruminate* Short Story Prize (issue 15, Spring 2010), and nominated for a Pushcart Prize by editor Brianna Van Dyke.

To the editors, thank you: Megan Ault Regnerus, Kerry Banazek, Brian Bedard, Michael Bowen, Claire Davis, Carol Edgarian, Nick Ehli, Dave Eggers, Eli Horowitz, Tom Jenks, Brian Kaufman, Amy Lowe, Joanna Manning, Jesse Nathan, Scott Peterson, M. M. M. Hayes, Kelli Russell Agodon, Annette Spaulding-Convy, and Brianna Van Dyke. You ask the great questions of life, and help us find our way.

ACKNOWLEDGMENTS

To those who burn like torches, I give love: to Jennifer, you are my beloved, you are my friend, you are the one my soul loves; to my wife's father, Fred Crowell, for your joy for life and God; to my dear friend Jonathan Johnson for your devotion to wilderness and truth; to James Welch for Fools Crow; to A. B. Guthrie Jr. for The Big Sky; to Mary Oliver for Thirst; and to Sherman Alexie for War Dances. Viktor Frankl said what is to give light must endure burning. Thank you for taking me into the fire.

To those whose quiet power transforms people, I give my heart's blessing: to my three miracles, Natalya Alexis, Ariana Alexis, and Isabella Alexis for being the defenders of humankind; to my mom and dad, Sandy and Tom Ferch, for the light of forgiveness; to my brother, Kral, for your brotherhood, for basketball, and for rising up and throwing down; to my wife's mother, Susie Crowell, for your healing presence; to my family's intellectual and spiritual father, Dr. Bernie Tyrrell, SJ, for continually opening us to the generosity of God—you are strength and peace.

To those whose gifts astound me I give thanks: to my good friend Jess Walter for your kindness and selfless vision; to poet Christopher Howell for Light's Ladder; to Eli Horowitz and Dave Eggers at McSweeney's for believing; to Emily Forland for seeing before it came to be; to Robert Boswell for selecting American Masculine; to Michael Collier for the call; to Steve Woodward for your care and discerning eye; and to Fiona McCrae for your devotion to the life of the artist, and for the great honor it has been to be influenced by the Graywolf family.

BREAD LOAF AND THE BAKELESS PRIZES

The Katharine Bakeless Nason Literary Publication Prizes were established in 1995 to expand the Bread Loaf Writers' Conference's commitment to the support of emerging writers. Endowed by the LZ Francis Foundation, the prizes commemorate Middlebury College patron Katharine Bakeless Nason and launch the publication career of a poet, fiction writer, and a creative nonfiction writer annually. Winning manuscripts are chosen in an open national competition by a distinguished judge in each genre. Winners are published by Graywolf Press.

2010 Judges

Arthur Sze
Poetry

Robert Boswell
Fiction

Jane Brox
Creative Nonfiction

Born and raised in Montana, SHANN RAY spent part of his childhood on the Northern Cheyenne reservation. He holds a PhD in psychology and a dual MFA in poetry and fiction. His work has appeared in *Poetry International, Northwest Review, Narrative,* and the anthology *The Better of McSweeney's, vol. 2.* He has served as a panelist of the National Endowment of the Humanities and a research psychologist for the Centers for Disease Control. He lives with his wife and three daughters in Spokane, Washington, where he teaches leadership and forgiveness studies at Gonzaga University.

Book design by Connie Kuhnz.
Composition by BookMobile Design and Publishing Services,
Minneapolis, Minnesota.
Manufactured by Versa Press on acid-free 30 percent
postconsumer wastepaper.